To David

All the

[illegible]

x

A British War Dance is the first novel from Lee Willmore. Lee was born and raised in the Sandwell area of the West Midlands and now resides in Kent. He has a keen interest in dance and the war time era, both of which were his inspiration for his story.

Dedication

This book is dedicated to my wife Keighley, who has always supported me and I love dearly. Also to my family for always believing in me.

Lee Willmore

A British War Dance

Austin Macauley Publishers™
London • Cambridge • New York • Sharjah

A CIP catalogue record for this title is available from the British Library.

ISBN 9781788486477 (Paperback)
ISBN 9781788486484 (Hardback)
ISBN 9781788486491 (E-Book)

www.austinmacauley.com

First Published (2018)
Austin Macauley Publishers Ltd™
25 Canada Square
Canary Wharf
London
E14 5LQ

Table of Contents

Chapter One

It was 1940, and the air was filled with the smoke of fallen rubble, gases from military action and pollution of a war that had only just begun. The streets of Birmingham changed from hustle and bustle to one that could only be described as an area broken from its own independence. The street curbs and pavements were filled with sandbags to protect houses and shops from what may happen if the enemy was to arrive. Every corner of Birmingham was continuously being patrolled by the armed forces. Wardens and walls on buildings were advertising for more men to join the army as the country needed as much support it could possibly get from the men that were able-bodied and not afraid of taking a life if someone was to confront them whilst battling in front-line experiences.

When the night of day fell, central Birmingham became an area where life seemed a little better as everyone danced, sang, socialised and went to the theatre to see shows in order to forget about what was going on in the world around them. It also helped them forget the constant reminder that their loved ones may never return from fighting for the country they loved. They spoke about their days and gossiped of who has not been seen in town for a while, how work has been affected due to bombings and of the things that had been stolen from their homes whilst air raid sirens were going off without them knowing. But more importantly, they spoke of love and friendship. These were the two bonds that held everyone's lives together. It was a way of showing no matter how bad life gets, you always have the good times in memory, and this was something that could not be taken away from anyone.

This brings you to my story, a story of dance, passion, love, sacrifice and friendship that all started in the year of 1940.

It all began on Monday 17 June, with Mrs Ashfield, sitting at home listening to the radio. She was a lady who was always dressed in clothes that she had amended herself from other garments which she owned, following sewing patterns that had been given to her by friends and relatives. Her hair was a medium brown and was always kept in a hairnet holding her curls together. Her skin was fair and she always wore little or no make-up as she did not like the idea of making herself look pretty since the death of her husband years before. All of her neighbours knew her, and she had a reputation of being a lovely lady who would do anything for someone if they asked.

It was late evening when she received a knock on the door by a British soldier, dressed smartly in his full attire and standing quite rigidly with an envelope under his arm. Opening the door, the sergeant started to talk to her in a deep voice:

"Hello Madam, my name is sergeant Payton, may I speak with Mrs Ashfield, please? I have an important telegram to give her regarding her two sons who are currently performing their duty in Germany at the moment. It is informing her that James is to return home after being discharged from military action." He handed the telegram over to her.

Mrs Ashfield replied with a worried expression on her face. "I am Mrs Ashfield, I hope my boys are okay."

The sergeant could tell that she was worried and as he looked through the door, he saw that her front room was filled with photos of the sons dressed in their uniforms before they left for Germany, along with lots of newspaper clippings of what was happening where her sons were currently based in service. The letters that had been sent home were nicely piled on top of each other on the living room table.

"May I come in, Mrs Ashfield?" Sergeant Payton said with a comforting tone of voice.

As he entered the house, the smell of a Lord Wooltons pie was entering the room, and he couldn't resist making a comment, "Your cooking skills smell exceptional Mrs Ashfield, I bet your family will enjoy what you have made them."

Mrs Ashfield blushed as her face went bright red and went to talk until she was interrupted by sergeant Payton once again.

"Now where was I? Oh that's right! The telegram about your two sons, all you need to know is written inside, and I will warn you, James will take a while to get back to some normality. I must go and take care of yourself, Mrs Ashfield, as this is a serious time we live in."

The sergeant left in a hurry when he saw some military vehicles go by quickly through the window, as this could be some important information he had been awaiting on, following some paperwork he received the day before. Mrs Ashfield closed the door and proceeded to sit down in her living room that was beautifully decorated with dark oak furniture, patterned wall paper and matching seating, which made it look all elegant.

As the sun began to fall, Mrs Ashfield sat on the sofa with the telegram in her hand, frightened to read what had happened, and it took minutes for her to pick up the courage to read what was written on it due to the questions going round and round in her mind. *Are they okay? Why are they returning? I don't want to know if something bad has happened, surely it could not have.* She finally got the courage to open it; she lit a candle and read the telegram aloud:

Mrs Ashfield,

I am writing today 16 June 1940, to advise you that your son James will be returning home after an event that occurred with James and Thomas Ashfield on 14 June. James and Thomas came face to face with a couple of German soldiers in one of the battle fields in Germany, Wilhelm (the leader) and Kurt (his brother). They had to make a quick decision on shooting the enemy to save their own lives. James shot Kurt in the head, killing him immediately. Outraged by what Wilhelm had seen, he then killed Thomas in the same way. James managed to escape, but since this date, he has not been able to keep a stable state of mind. Therefore, he is being returned to your care due to potential mental health issues, as we deem he is in no state of mind to carry on fighting at present. We would like to inform you that James may require some care as the memories of this event are still on his mind, and he will have outbursts randomly throughout the day which include not being able to rest and shouting during sleep when he is able to settle down. It is our recommendation that he sees a doctor if this gets worse.

We are very sorry for the loss of your son Thomas. The actions he has taken during his service have been outstanding and have made a difference to future lives of others and we thank him for all he has done.

James will be returning home at 19:00 hrs tomorrow and will not be returning to the army until we see fit.

Yours sincerely
General Banks
Head of the British Army.

Shocked by what she had read, Mrs Ashfield broke down in tears for the loss of her son that she knew nothing about until now. After a while, although the tears stopped, her heart felt broken but she managed to jump up onto her feet to start tidying the house in preparation for when James was to return home.

The Ashfield household was a nice home, consisting of a kitchen and dining room combined with flowery pastel colour wallpaper and dark mahogany furniture. The living room had a lovely feel to it. It had an open fire place with chopped wood sitting beside it ready to be burned on cold evenings; the walls were decorated with swirled patterns and photos of family, and in the corner of the room there was a record player with records of classical music and the current songs of the times. The house also had three bedrooms and an outside bathroom, which sat next to the garden with its flowers and vegetable patch, which was Mrs Ashfield's pride and joy. The most important part of the garden was an air raid shelter that was built by Mr Hale, a close friend of Mrs Ashfield. The shelter was frequently used when the sirens went off and was packed with essentials that Mrs Ashfield thought were necessary if the enemy were to attack and if she was going to be in there for long periods of times. Once she had finished tidying the house, she put on one of her records and fell asleep looking forward to her son's return.

Morning came, and Mrs Ashfield awoke to the sound of her alarm clock at 06:00 hours, opened the curtains and looked out the window and said to herself, "My boy is coming home today, how I have missed him, both of them. I must get ready."

Mrs Ashfield quickly walked upstairs and got into her best dress, a full circle floral number in light blue, yellow and white made out of cotton, which she hand stitched a few months ago in preparation of her sons' return. Her shoes were a light brown brogue in a size 4 and her hair was done in an updo and had so much product in it that it would simply not move. She sang at the top of her voice and opened up the windows to make sure that there was fresh air going through the place. Mrs Ashfield hurried downstairs, put a plate of fresh-made cakes on her fine china plates and used some of her ration coupons on some nice food. She went into the garden and picked some of the flowers that were worthy for display and put them in a vase on the coffee table in the living room.

"There, that will do," she said, "I'm ready for his return home."

She sat and waited for the door to go. Hours had passed and still no sign of them. The sky was turning from blue to black, and the black metal street lights of Birmingham began slowly turning on, one by one, lighting up the path ways of the cobbled streets. The bars were starting to empty after a busy day's trading and all began to go silent, so silent that you could hear leaves of all the trees nearby, cars and military vehicles patrolling the streets and wardens making sure that everything was okay. All of a sudden, there were three loud knocks on the door with a whispering of a voice, this voice was of her son James who had a very deep voice that was hard to miss.

James was looking at the door number of his mother's house as he was talking to himself quietly, "I'm not sure that ma'am will be awake at this hour, it is after all 23:00 hours, and here I am making so much noise." If anyone was to walk by, they would have thought James had been sent from a mental home.

He continued whispering, "After all this time, I do not think mother will really be bothered about when or what time I was returning home, after all, the head of the army has already been saying that I will be arriving today. If I don't go in now, it will be tomorrow, and she will only be worrying. How am I going to tell her about my dear brother being killed? I miss him so much!"

When James stopped talking, he could hear his mother coming towards the front of the house. The front door opened and Mrs Ashfield couldn't believe her eyes. They started to fill with tears, she was lost for words and was so happy James was safe and sound. James dropped his bags and coats onto the floor and moved towards his mother with open arms to give her the biggest hug that she deserved. They both said with smiles on their faces, "I love you!"

They both went indoors and shut the door behind them to catch up on what had happened when James and Thomas were in service.

Chapter Two

James headed straight upstairs to put all the clothes and bags he had brought back with him into his room. He looked around the rooms to remind himself of what stuff had been left behind when he left for war. James's room had grey walls and furnishings to match its colour; shelves had articles of theatre shows and plays along with handwritten scripts he wrote for a hobby, as well as clippings of musical notes as he was into dance and music.

James was 22 years old and a dancer at heart. Since a teenager, he was into Charleston and ballet, and had taught himself how to dance both of these styles in the secrecy of his bedroom as he did not know how his family would take to him doing such things, as most of his friends were into sports. James also had a brown wooden piano in the corner of his room with pages of musical notes he had composed on top of it, all scattered from the last time he played them. James was 5'9 with mousy brown hair that was smartly parted to the right and had a shiny look to it. He had a slim chest with a good figure. His icy cold blue eyes looked like they could draw you in if you were to stare at them long enough. He always dressed smartly when not in uniform and always made sure he looked presentable, especially when he was about to do the dancing he thought highly of.

Thomas's room was now just a shrine to his life. The room was very plain and everything was neatly stored away as he was a very private man, the only thing displayed on the wall was a picture of a house in a quiet countryside. Some would say this was like his personality as he always kept things to himself. Thomas was 5'6, with black hair and dark, mysterious eyes that always seemed to get darker the more you looked at them. His figure was skinny as he did not seem to have much of an appetite either. It was hard to believe he was no longer with them.

After dropping the bags in his room and spending some time remembering his brother, he made his way downstairs, picking up the courage to discuss what had happened to his brother on that dreadful night in Germany. As he approached the living room, he could see his mother was still crying on the sofa. James sat down next to her and took her hands as he began to speak, "So how have you been?" asked James.

"Worried, that's how! I don't know where you have been, I was constantly thinking that something bad may have happened to you both and then I have some soldier knock on my door with this telegram, I can't believe Thomas is no longer with us! I understand you may not want to discuss what happened as I know it has been hard for you, but I'm sorry Son, I need to know!" Mrs Ashfield's voice was cracking up from being so upset.

Whilst she was speaking, James thought for a while of a nice reply, but couldn't think of an easy or nice way to put it to one of the people he loved so dearly.

James decided he had to tell his Mother how it was, so he started to tell her the story of how it happened.

"It was the 14 June and we had been deployed to a battlefield near the German capital. I was told to team up with a group of soldiers that Thomas had also been assigned to. It was night time and we had not eaten for hours, and every soldier was feeling tired and weak. The skies were filled with smoke from the bombs and gun fire that was going on in the distance. Thomas and I were told that we were going to be one of the first batches of soldiers to go forward on the front line, and being brothers we felt an immense comfort in going into battle together.

"We were halfway along the land we had been given to fight on when Thomas noticed we were being followed by two German soldiers. As we were next to these two men, they had the most frightened look on their faces that you could imagine and we both noticed they both had grey and black uniforms that were ripped in certain places. One of the German soldiers was called Kurt, and he too was with his brother called Wilhelm. We knew their names as there was a moment of discussion between them, I had spent many nights in my spare time learning the basics of their language. They were both pointing their guns at us, ready to pull the trigger. He hesitated, and I knew that if I did not shoot at Kurt soon, we were the ones at risk, so I had to make a fast decision, and I shot him in the head. I didn't want to, but it's what we were ordered to do. I just stared at him for a moment, lying there surrounded by a pool of his own blood.

"As I did, I heard another shot next to me along with a tug on my sleeve a second later; Wilhelm had shot

Thomas near his heart and he had fallen to the ground. He started to shake, and his last words to me were that I should do what makes me happy and to tell you that he loved you too. I have brought back home his watch which he wanted you to have when he was to return home. I looked up, but Wilhelm was in the distance running away, if he stayed I would have made him pay for killing Thomas, but it was too late.

"I now wish I didn't go to war, and I keep thinking how different things would have been if I didn't shoot, but they were the orders we were given from the British army and I had to do it or I would be considered a coward."

Tears started to flow from his eyes as he continued, "The questions going through my mind at the time were: why did I have to lose my brother? Did the German soldier have any children? Will his family be informed of what has just happened? So I made a decision and went through the soldier's belongings in his pockets and took this from his jacket."

James put a book on the coffee table with a photo inside it, along with what looked like journal entries of what he had seen during service and an address with his ID number within the German army.

James started to talk more quietly, "Every night since, I have had terrible nightmares and flashbacks of this event. I can't sleep and I can't eat properly... Even if I managed to, I would not be able to keep it down due to sickness. But more importantly, if it wasn't for Thomas, I don't know if I would have made it back home myself."

Mrs Ashfield put her arms around James and said, "You did the best for your brother, you did what you needed to do, and no one will ever think badly of what you have done, especially me! You're fighting for your country, and you did a bloody good job of it too! So please don't put yourself down or through any more pain, you're a good guy and always will be! I too will miss Thomas and don't know how long it will take my heart to mend, but I will always hold him close to my heart. Life must go on, and my dear now that you are home, we will be fine. You have to do what makes you happy from now on."

James gave a small smile as he started to speak, "I just don't understand why this war has started, why the German army has decided that it needs to happen, I wish it would just end. Until I am better, I'm going to carry on with what I loved before this war all began… my dancing. I'm going to push myself to the best dancer I can be, either on stage or as a hobby, either way, it's happening. All I'm asking is that you support me with my dreams, and I'm sorry if I keep you up at night Mother, I just can't stop the flashbacks of what has happened when I go to bed, and if I talk or shout in the middle of the night, just ignore me. Good night, Mother."

James kissed his mother on the cheek and went upstairs with Carrot Cake he took on a plate from the kitchen, passing his mother standing near the living room window with her head in her hands. At the top of the stairs were pictures of the Ashfield family on the wall, all the photos from left to right were of every generation of the family in their nicest clothes and uniforms. James stared at the family group photo he liked most, which was of himself, Thomas, Mrs Ashfield and his dad Kevin before he died.

Kevin was a fine, well-liked, professional gentleman who got on well with everyone. He supported you no matter what your problem was and loved working in his store room; he was also known to like working on cars now and then and repaired them as part-time job on the side of his normal profession. Unfortunately, James and Thomas knew little of him, as he died when they were only years or months old, but whenever they felt down about something, this is the photo they looked at. James stared at the photo a moment longer and went to his room.

Around an hour later, Mrs Ashfield went to his room to make sure he was okay.

"James, are you awake? I have been thinking of ways to help you get better, and I think you need to get a job to take your mind off things, especially if you're to try and get over this experience you have had in Germany."

James nodded back as his mother carried on talking, "So what is it right now that would make you happy, what is the one thing you want to do as a job?"

James thought about this and replied, "I want to dance. I know it sounds crazy and I know you don't think highly of it, but all my worries go away when I dance. I know this will be a shock to you, but I have been teaching myself ballet for many years." He started to smile as he carried on, "When I dance ballet, I feel like no one can stop me, and I think that if a part became available in the theatre or entertainment industry in this big world we live in, then I would go for it and see what other people think of my abilities."

Mrs Ashfield looked at him and said, "That is ridiculous, people will laugh at you! A grown man comes back from the army to join a ballet, we would be the talk of the town and people will laugh at us! For God's sake, what would your father think? If you do this, you are no son of mine, and I will disown you!"

Mrs Ashfield left the room, slamming the door behind her, whilst James tucked into the cake he took with him to his bedroom before turning the light out to try and get some rest.

Mrs Ashfield sat down in her living room with a cup of tea, in shock, thinking about how her son just told her that he liked to do ballet, and how she meant what she said about removing James from the family if he was to go down this route. She picked up the German soldier's diary that James had left on the coffee table and flicked through the pages that were full of writing she didn't fully understand, as she had never seen the German language on paper before. She got to the photograph in the book which was in black and white of a young woman posing perfectly. The woman looked dignified and high class, wearing what looked like a long evening dress with a head dress. On the back of the photograph was a date and a name 'Pauline'. Mrs Ashfield decided it was wrong to go through her son's stuff without him knowing, so she put the photo back in the book on the coffee table and went to bed.

Morning came and James was already downstairs looking through the newspaper that had been released the day before. The main headline read 'More British Soldiers Sent Overseas', but James did not read this article in full, as the thought of it concerned him. He skipped straight to the business, entertainment and job column, and after 10 minutes of looking through it, he saw an advertisement for auditions for a new ballet show called ‘A British War Dance’. The advert read ‘Ballet show for 8 weeks, only starting on 1 November, 1940. Cast members needed: Ten females. Also, one stage manager needed. Auditions and applications this Saturday, 10:00 hours at Birmingham Town Hall. James kept looking and looking at this advert contemplating whether or not if he should go for the stage manager role as he was unable to audition as a dancer.

“What do I have to lose?” he said to himself and began to get his bag packed to go into town, knowing that this could either be a good move or a bad one.

James shouted upstairs to his mother in an excited tone, “Just going out, be back soon.” He was not sure if his mom would be up yet.

He left the house with his hands in his jacket, looking at the floor as he walked just in case he bumped into anyone he knew. The weather outside was cold, windy and the sky was grey, with no clouds in sight. In the distance, all that could be heard were vehicles and planes going about their day-to-day business, protecting the city and people travelling to and from work. James was five minutes away from the Town Hall when he bumped into John Dudley who lived across the street, an old friend from school who joined the navy as soon as he left his education. As much as James kept his head down and hands in his pockets, he just couldn’t avoid being seen by him.

John was 6’2 and had a well-built figure, due to him being very good at sports when he was in school. His eyes were golden green, and his hair was black and slick with a side parting. He had a stubbly beard which itched like hell and always wore his petty officers uniform with pride that was given to him when he first joined the navy. The shoulder bag he carried had newspapers and paperwork, along with a lunch box of old sandwiches he forgot to throw away when he was working from home.

“James, what are you doing home? I thought you were fighting for our country in Germany, or were you not good enough?” John was talking loudly so everyone else could hear.

“I was discharged from my duty, thank you very much. My officer told me that I was allowed to come home as we were no longer required in action until further notice.” James knew that this was a twist on the true story, and that if he kept on talking, he would slip up with what really happened.

“Oh so how about your brother, is he still out there?” John said this whilst stroking his tie. He was wearing with his uniform to prove a point. James knew what he was trying to do and was conscious that if he did not make tracks soon, he would miss his opportunity at the Town Hall.

“I really must go John, I have an application I need to hand in, was nice seeing you. Bye.” James said this in what he thought was quite a rude manner but in fact, was just as polite as normal considering the circumstances.

He finally approached the Town Hall, which was located on Victoria Square, a large grey stone building that was built with high standards for such events. Outside the building, there was a queue of ladies which went very far out of the door, full of dancers wanting to be in the spotlight of the show they called a once in a life time experience. All of the women were dressed in their best outfits, from suits and dresses to anything else they deemed to be worthy of being seen in for such an important audition.

James noticed that all of them were holding their ballet pointe shoes which varied from being brand new to used and repaired. The only thing going through James's mind was how much he wanted to be involved and how he would like to be dancing with the ten successful applicants but knew this would never happen. As he joined the back of the queue, he could hear the women starting to talk about him, as he was the only male who made an appearance for the stage manager role. Eventually, the conversation between the women died down, until the woman that stood in front of him, who had put way too much make-up on, started to talk to him.

"So what makes you think you have a chance of managing such a masterpiece of a production?" as she spoke, she sounded stuck up.

"Well, I'm a dancer myself and have read many articles and a book about the history of some ballet choreographers. I might just have a chance, after all, there is only myself applying for this role." James thought he had given such a good reply that she may leave him alone.

"We will see, after all, you do have to prove yourself in this type of business," she turned her back around, and you could tell that everyone around her was beginning to get annoyed with her too.

The line started to move again, and before James knew it, he wrote his name on a list at the front desk and was told to go to the waiting room near the stage. When he got there, he was taken aback by the beauty of architecture and how big the place was without anyone sitting in the stalls. The stage area was a lovely wooden pine that had scuff marks of where previous people had danced or acted. The ceiling had wonderful visuals hanging from it such as the tops of trees and clouds, the backdrops were of different scenes like night time, day time and others that were going to be used during the production.

A moment later, he heard a voice call out names and an announcement: "Caroline, Sharon, Sam and Kayleigh… you are next to audition and please remember this is your only chance to impress us. Please make sure that you use the ballet moves given to you when you logged your name at the front desk when you first entered the building." The announcement came from a lady called Barbara, who had a stern look to her and you knew not to mess around when she was close by, as this was her show.

The classical music started, and the four girls began to dance the routine that they were provided with, and everyone watching noticed how competitive it was getting. Each dancer needed to keep their posture as they moved and also needed to make sure that they did not come out of the space they were provided with.

James could not stop watching, but his eyes were fixed on one person in particular, and that person was Sam. Sam had blue eyes, long red hair that was curled and smartly done make-up. She was slim and wore a cocktail dress that swung when she twirled. James knew she was the most beautiful girl he had ever seen. All of a sudden, the dancers' auditions approached their last move, a double turn on pointes, and James was still watching Sam. He noticed that when she went to do the last turn, she stumbled and twisted her foot; he could tell she was going to struggle. James knew from reading past papers that the general rules of such a production were that if you did not complete the full routine, you were graded very low. With this in mind, he rushed onto the stage next to Sam, picked up her arm and put it on his shoulder, walking around her, tip-toeing on his feet whilst her bad leg was elevated in the air. The other dancers started to whisper.

Sam looked at James and said, "Why did you do that? You risked your own interview and reputation for me; no one has ever treated me in such a way before! What is your name?"

James gave a slight smile and thought about his reply carefully, "I have never been so captivated by a woman's beauty and watching you dance was breathtaking, it was worth helping you! My name is James; I better go as I will be called soon. Do you fancy meeting me for a drink later in Wood Green Hotel at 20:00 hours?" He smiled at her as he looked into her eyes.

"Sure, see you there, I will look forward to it," she replied whilst smiling back at him.

All of sudden, James was called for his interview by David, Barbara's husband who was a lot nicer. The room he was taken to was small and had little character to it, and it smelt a little damp. He got questioned on why he should be picked for the manager role and what made him better than the other applicants who were going to be interviewed, as well as what his hobbies were. At the end of the interview, James was told that he would be contacted if he was successful, and that news spreads fast within the business for helping someone he did not know, he was highly thought of for doing it.

James left the Town Hall to go home feeling nervous as he could not stop thinking of the girl he had briefly danced with and that they were soon to meet for the first time. He started to think about what he should wear, how awkward it might turn out to be, should he have helped her during her audition, and what if he had ruined her chances of being picked for the show?

He finally got home and went straight to his room, sat down at his piano and began playing some classical music to help take his mind off his first date that was going to happen that evening. Outside his room's door, Mrs Ashfield stood quietly and listened as he played the romantic tune with his eyes closed. Mrs Ashfield thought that for the first time that James was in love. She walked away and went downstairs again, leaving James to play his piano in the privacy of his room.

Chapter Three

The sun started to go down and a mist of fog began to beckon among the streets of Birmingham town, and people were getting ready for a social gathering in one of the few public houses that served locally produced drinks and snacks with varied entertainment throughout the night. James was suited head to toe in a black suit jacket and wide-legged swing trousers which had a thin blue and white pinstripe on it. Underneath his jacket was a white, smartly ironed shirt, blue tie and his black brogues which he had owned for many years, fitted firmly around his feet. This was one of his dad's old suits, which he used to wear to work, and it was handed down to James when he passed away, along with a silver bracelet that was one of his favourites. He sprayed some cologne by 'Goring', a well-known fragrance that was deemed an expensive brand on the high street, and was then ready for his night out at the hotel with the girl he had fallen for earlier that day.

James was so nervous, he started to sweat a little; he could not stay still and was watching the clock. The time at this point was 19:00 hours, and his journey to the Wood Green Hotel was about 30 minutes' drive away, so he decided that he would make tracks. He picked up the courage and made the first step outside his front door when an air raid siren began to go off and Mrs Ashfield was shouting from the garden for him to hurry into the shelter. Disappointed, he ran to the shelter, made his way into the tiny room and sat down on one of the benches that were placed in there to make longer periods of time more comfortable. After a short period of sitting in silence, Mrs Ashfield decided she would try and lighten the mood if she could.

"Going somewhere tonight, James? It's not often we see you dressed so smart!" Mrs Ashfield was laughing a little as she said this.

"Yes, I'm meeting someone I met today whilst I was out at the town hall," James was trying not to say much about the matter, as he was on edge about this as it was.

"Hang on, wasn't that the place they were auditioning for the new ballet production?" she added.

"Yes it is, I applied for the stage manager role, and I will hopefully hear back from them in due course," James stood up as the siren had stopped and all had seemed a little calmer outside. "I must go," he said as he ran from the shelter to his car in the driveway of the house, whilst his mother had an angry look upon her face.

His car was a lovely light-grey colour with light-brown leather interior and a wooden dashboard. The car was clean, tidy and the back seats had magazines from years ago sitting neatly in a pile just in case he ever got stuck somewhere in traffic. James got inside the car and turned the ignition key to the left of the steering wheel when a loud noise came from the engine as he started to pull off the driveway. James's hands started to shake and he was starting to get a little breathless, the last time he felt like this was the day he was fighting with the army. He began to sing his favourite wartime song to keep his nerves at bay.

He was about ten minutes away from the Wood Green Hotel when he heard a loud bang come from the distance; it went again. The noises were one similar to when he was in Germany; they reminded him of how he was and the things he saw. This was making him feel sick in the stomach, so much so that the car swerved slightly. A short while later, he pulled himself together and approached the car park sign that was hanging on a metal fence that separated the hotel from the street and its grounds.

The car park was small and only had a few cars parked far away from each other, and the corners of the car park had small plant pots with pretty looking flowers in them to make the place look a little more colourful.

James parked up and sat there for a while looking at his watch as he was early but before he knew it, the time had come to meet Sam. He started to walk towards the revolving glassed entrance doors that had silver plating to the edges, and the panels were of a fine oak wood with glass windows that were neatly etched with the name of the hotel on them. He walked through feeling quite posh that he was in such a grand-looking place, and before he knew it, he was standing in the reception area of the hotel where people waited for their visitors. The hotel reception had a red carpet, with a black rug that led a short way from the reception door, its walls were a cream and gold colour with a faint pattern that was quite hard to see unless you looked at it for a short period of time. The reception desk stood at an angle in the corner and was manned by a man called Jason Ryan, who was wearing his hotel uniform, which was black trousers, white shirt and a green waistcoat with a name badge pinned onto it.

"Good evening Sir, my name is Jason. Is there anything I may assist you with?" he was standing with his arms behind his back.

"I'm waiting for a friend to arrive, she should be here soon," James replied politely.

"Very well, if you need anything please do not hesitate to come see me at the desk in the corner, hope you enjoy your visit to Wood Green Hotel." He walked away and went to greet the next customer.

A moment later, Sam came walking through the door with her hair curled and perfectly done make-up. She wore a dress that was checked in turquoise and white, and wore pale blue shoes with small heels so she did not look too tall with what she was wearing.

"Hi James, it's lovely to see you again. Shall we go for a drink in the bar upstairs? I have lots to ask you!" she paused and waited for him to reply.

"Certainly but before we do, can I say how nice it is to meet you again after our brief encounter earlier today." James was looking straight into her eyes and continued to talk, "How was your journey? Hope it was pleasant." James was trying not to be too questioning as he spoke.

She smiled and nodded as they started to walk up the grand staircase of the hotel that led to the bar area upstairs, but as they did, they were both trying to look at each other discretely, so they didn't notice. They approached the top of the stairs and went into the bar and there were not many people at all dining apart from the residents who had booked to stay that night. They got some gin and coke from the bar, then James suggested sitting at a table with two chairs in the corner of the room that was next to a statue as it looked like a private place to drink. They slowly walked over to sit down.

James pulled out a chair from underneath and said, "After you." They both sat down and sipped their drinks at the same time. Sam was starting to think of a nice way to start a conversation without it being awkward and as she did, she started rummaging through her bag until she found an envelope she was looking for and placed it on the table.

She began to talk, "James about today… I just wanted to let you know I am truly grateful for what you did for me. No one has ever treated me with such respect before, especially when they do not even know me. What makes you so different from the others?" she stopped talking whilst she had a thoughtful look on her face.

"In all honesty, when I saw you dancing during your audition, I just could not take my eyes off you; I was fixed. You looked so beautiful, and you just captivated me as soon as you started your first move on your pointes," James gave a little sigh before he continued to talk, "Then I saw you get to one of the last double turns and noticed your footwork was a little out of place and then you started to stumble. I couldn't bear the thought of you injuring yourself, especially during an audition, so I thought I would help you finish the full routine."

Sam couldn't help but smile and replied back in a subtle voice, "But how did you learn to dance like that?

For a guy to know how to dance ballet and even more so when they do not know a routine with what was to happen next in my audition was a little outstanding. I was shocked and very impressed!" Sam stopped talking as she thought if she was to carry on, he might leave.

James replied back to her with a smile on his face, "People assume that being a guy means we are not interested in dancing and it's all about more manly stuff. For me, this was not the case, but I did it in the privacy of my own room when I was growing up. When I had the opportunity to dance, I danced! When I was feeling at my lowest, I just got up on my feet and began to learn something new. I started with Charleston, then went on to ballet, and I have never regretted it. That's why I applied for stage manager for the production today and danced with you when you were doing the double turn. I just want to be involved in any way I can to show what I am capable of."

Sam smiled, "Well, I wanted to let you know that thanks to you, I got the lead role in the production. I hope we can be more than friends, as I too have started to have feelings for you." She looked at her drink as she swirled it around, awaiting his reply.

"I think that is a delightful idea, as I feel the same way." His face went red as he was very happy that she had asked him into a relationship. James looked at his watch and saw that he needed to make a move home because he was due to get up early the next morning. They both walked back down to the entrance, where they exchanged kisses and good byes, and Sam was still holding onto the letter she pulled out of her bag earlier.

"Oh I almost forgot, Barbara knew I was seeing you tonight and wanted me to hand you a letter. I have no idea what it is, but she said to open it when you got home, I must be off. Good night, my love."

James took the envelope from her as she started to walk away to go home, thinking what could be written on the inside, but he decided he would read it when he got home. He ran to his car and got inside, smiled at himself in his mirror and started his return journey to see what the future held.

He pulled up outside his home, gathered his things and went indoors. He pulled a candle out of a drawer of a cabinet and lit it carefully, walking through to the dining room table where he put it in one of the candle holders. He sat down and held the envelope that had nicely written handwriting that looked as though it was used with the finest ink. He looked left, then right to make sure he was alone when he was to open a letter so important it could change his life and even make him happy. He carefully put his finger under the lip of the envelope and began to open it with care. James took a deep breath and began to read the letter:

Dear Mr J Ashfield,

Thank you for your visit to Birmingham Town Hall, applying for the role of Stage Manager for our upcoming production.

We were very impressed with your application, and you had all the qualities in which we were looking for. But unfortunately, you have been unsuccessful at this time.

A person with such attributes and the ability to dance ballet in a professional manner, whilst risking their own application to help another is outstanding to see. It is with this in mind that I am changing the direction of this production and would like to offer you a new role I have created in the hope you will agree to it.

This role is a lead male ballet dancer who goes by the name of 'Stephen' alongside the lady we have chosen to play the female lead. We hope you find this acceptable, and if you are agreeable, then please come and see me on Monday morning, 13:00 at Birmingham Town Hall.

I hope to speak soon.

Kind regards,

Barbara

James was in shock but knew what his answer would be straightaway, there was no question about it. His dream was finally coming true, a lead role dancing in front of public on a daily basis, the lead girl was his new partner Sam, and most importantly, he was happy. He put the letter back in its envelope, so he knew where it was and went upstairs to his room, closed the curtains and got ready for bed knowing that in the next few days he had a new adventure in front ready for him.

The next day, Mrs Ashfield was downstairs listening to the radio about the recent news of what was happening in Germany and how the British government were trying to defend its people, not like they would give much away as it had to be kept secret from the German army. Announcements and updates were about the recent cut backs and rations that were going to be put in place, and as they were, Mrs Ashfield was writing them down in a bit of tatty paper that she had found lying around the house so she could keep the information safe. Moments later, James appeared in the kitchen about to make some breakfast, and his mother looked at him as though he was acting differently.

"So what has you up so early this morning and why does your face look happy? You have never been a morning person!" Mrs Ashfield was digging for the recent gossip.

"I have to go meet someone today about a letter I received in the last day or so, and the news is the best I have received in a long time. I didn't even have my usual fit last night, so must have been what I needed," his reply was of an upbeat nature.

"Can I see the letter?" Mrs Ashfield held out her right hand, as if it was more of an order than a question.

James went upstairs, got the letter and proceeded back to the kitchen where his mother was still sitting there with her arm in the same position when she asked for the letter. "There you go, but please understand that I'm accepting this role, no matter what you think!" Mrs Ashfield began to read the letter looking more and more serious as she got to the end and as she did, she slammed the letter on the table with both her hands as she stood up at the same time. The loud bang followed by his mother's reaction had James shaking again with the images of what happened in Germany coming to the front of his mind again.

"I will not allow you to go ahead with this, James, after all the support I gave you whilst we were away fighting for our country, and after all the things I have done for you, you're going to make our family a laughing stock… A joke!" Mrs Ashfield's voice was getting louder.

"You said the day I returned, that you would want me to be happy and to do what I love. You should support me! And ballet is the one dance style I love, and that's why I applied at the town hall for a job as a stage manager. So I could be part of a new production in any way I could, and the rest you know yourself from the letter!" James replied in a warbled tone as his mother was starting to get a little closer to him.

"But a man doing ballet, how ridiculous! Do you not realise what impact this could have on our family? What your father would think! What people may say about you behind your back, especially the guys you worked with in the army! How did you think I was going to take the news? I'm sorry James, the way I see it, you either turn the job down or you are no longer my son, and you leave this house right now until you come to your senses!" Mrs Ashfield was pointing to the front door, awaiting the response.

"Well, I guess this is it then, my happiness is worth a million times more than other people's thoughts, especially those of a mother who should be sticking by me no matter what. You're just like the others, I guess this is it then, I'm now without a mother too! I will be staying at the hotel if you change your views about what I'm doing. Either way, it's happening."

James grabbed a few supplies and slammed the door behind him as his mother shouted: "You are no son of mine!"

Chapter Four

At midday, James found himself parking his car in a cold, shadowed narrow street just minutes' walk from Birmingham Town Hall, the doorways were ones of the back of people's houses and smelt badly of tobacco. If you were to carry on down this road for miles, you would come across the canals of Birmingham. These were currently used to take important military supplies and sand bags for the war up or down stream; it was also nice to look at on a calm sunny day. James locked his belongings in the back of his car to check in to a hotel later that day, after all, he wasn't going home anytime soon after the argument earlier. He picked up his shoulder bag which contained the letter and started to walk to the hall. Although he was early, he knew it was better to be, as being late would not be good. James stood outside the entrance until there were ten minutes to go, then knocked on the door whilst making sure his hair was perfectly parted in his reflection in the door window. The door opened, and it was Barbara looking as thoughtful as ever:

"Ahhh James, you got my letter, please come in, and we can talk. I trust you approved, and we're happy with what I had written?"

James nodded as they walked through the building to the damp room he was originally interviewed in and in the background, there was an orchestra practising its classical pieces, but the place seemed a lot more relaxed. They both sat down at the desk which was now placed with a Bakelite telephone, a ceramic jug filled with water and two nicely designed glasses that stood next to a pile of discoloured papers. Barbara started the conversation as James waited and wondered about how to start a conversation that did not come across as over the top and too excitable.

"So about my letter James, how do you feel about the opportunity to dance alongside our leading female dancer, Sam? She told me the other day she would be meeting with you to discuss the events later that day. I too was lost for words that you would give up your own interview for a complete stranger! There must have been something in the back of your head that made you choose to act on your actions." Barbara rested her head in the hands whilst waiting for the reply.

"As you know, I met with Sam that evening and I told her my feelings, and the future for us both now looks very promising. I got home that night and opened your letter that was passed to me, the only reply I have to give you is that it would be a great honour to dance in your production, and I owe you for creating a new role that you saw fit for me. I have always had a passion for dance, especially when it comes to ballet, and I am glad you acknowledged my potential."

He took a sip of water as Barbara continued. "But how does a man of your age, let alone having a past in the military, know such moves without me providing you with the routine? That I find outstanding and that is why I created your role." She smiled as if his reply would be one to remember.

"All I ever wanted in my lifetime was to set an example that men can dance if they put their minds to it, that it is not always danced by one gender. If I can dance this production with passion and get others like me interested, I will die a happy man!" James took a deep breath as he said this quite quickly without taking a breath.

Barbara was still smiling, "This is why I sent the letter and asked you to be part of the production using the new role I created; we can expect this show to be big and more importantly, a lot more interesting now that we have you on board. Remember, to succeed you need passion, and with passion it leads to bigger and better things!" She stood up holding a contract for James to sign that she had typed up that day and handed it to him with a fountain pen. "Then if you fully accept, please sign at the bottom of the contract to say you agree to the terms."

James started to read the terms that were bullet pointed on the contract:

- Your role: Lead Male Ballet dancer (to dance with Sam our female Lead Ballet Dancer)
- Costume will be fitted and your responsibility to not tear or damage. Any damage and repairs will be at the cost of the dancer.
- Every day you will be required for dance practice for 4 hours starting at 11:00 and to

prepare for the nightly show from 17:00 each evening.

- The Production will be for eight weeks only Monday – Saturday evenings, when curtains open at 19:00 and curtains close 22:00.
- Payment will be given in person at the end of each Saturday night.
- If you are unable to dance for any reason, then you must inform a member of management immediately so a stand-in can be arranged.
- We are not responsible for loss of property, and it is up to you to keep safe at all times.
- No relationships between cast members are allowed at any stage, and if found to be, you will be dismissed.

James finished reading the finer small print on the back, and hesitated slightly as he could not think of ending his new relationship with Sam but also did not want to end his dream, so he decided to accept the contract and signed his name as the possibility of another role coming to him like this was very slim. He passed the paperwork to Barbara and thanked her for the opportunity whilst turning to the door to go find somewhere nearby to stay, when Barbara started to speak again,

"Thank you once again, James. First rehearsal is tonight at 19:00 with a costume fitting, please make sure you are here early enough as my sister is going to start on yours tonight and requires your measurements!"

"I will certainly make sure I am here in plenty of time and will not let you down, I promise," he replied in an excited tone and started to make his way out the building back to his car to find somewhere to stay for the foreseeable future.

At this point, he knew there were not many places to stay and started to think of other options. The Wood Green Hotel was too far away to be travelling every day, but as he looked down the road, he noticed a paper pinned to a wooden post advertising a small family-run hotel with rooms available, so he pulled it down to take with him. This was five minutes away, so he made his travels following the directions given, when he finally approached a nice-looking house with a red stone front with a lovely green plant that had grown up its walls to give a nice feeling about it.

The hotel was called Mesty Croft Hotel, named after a school teacher who used to live there prior to the current owners. The windows were painted white, and there was a handmade sign in the windows saying: 'Rooms Available – Enquire Within'. James got his belongings, made his way inside and noticed that the décor was dark throughout and did not have much light passing through. The front desk was made of dark wood with a dark green sign hanging above it saying, 'Reception'. On the desk, there was a bell that was made from cheap silver for people to press if no one was around. The place was silent, and no one was to be found, so James rang the bell and waited for someone to come along and help him.

Eventually, a gentleman came from a small office next to the reception desk; he was tall, with brown hair and eyes, but also looked like he had been having an argument with someone out back. He introduced himself.

"Good afternoon, what I can do for you today?" his voice was deep and had a strong accent to it.

"I would like to enquire as to whether you have a single room available on long term basis please, as I will be working not far from here, and also I would be grateful if you could advise me on the costs too please?" James asked the question as if he was new in town.

"Week prices for one person including breakfast are at 2 pounds and a shilling at the moment, and we have one room left, I would get it whilst I can with the recent events of buildings going down. Would you like it?" He placed the key on the desk whilst he was waiting for a decision.

As James knew there were not many places to stay at the moment, he had to agree. He was also curious to find out more about the owners and started to ask the question, "I would like to go ahead if that's okay with you?" he put his week's payment on the desk whilst he waited for the owner to answer him.

"Thank you, sir, we hope you enjoy your stay. There is your key, and please keep the noise to a minimum though, as we like our residents to rest well during times like these! Oh and your name?" The owner wanted to end the conversation as quick as he could and made a hand gesture as to get James to hurry up.

"James Ashfield and may I take yours?" He bent down to pick up his stuff whilst waiting to hear what this man's name was, and when he stood back up, the man had left the room. Despite how rude James thought this man was being, he looked at his room number, which was attached to his key; it had 'Room 8' written on it. James followed the sign on the wall indicating where his temporary resting place would be until things at home got sorted. He finally got to his door, which looked like it could do with a bit of paint as it was marked and well-worn, but proceeded to put his key in the lock and open the door.

As he walked into the room, he looked around whilst placing his belongings in certain places. The walls were white, and the curtains and bedding were of a deep colour, the carpet was clean apart from some parts that had stains on them from when previous guests had spilt their drinks on the floor. The desk in the corner had a clock and desk lamp sitting upon it, and the window overlooked the street that was once again full of local people going about their everyday activities. James got settled before getting dressed into some more appropriate clothing to go to his rehearsal later that day, which he knew would hold lots of exciting challenges and test his dedication regarding his level of dance.

After he was dressed and ready to leave, he suddenly remembered that he needed to meet Sam at 17:00 hours, and only had minutes to go before he met her at the park near the Town Hall. He began to leave the hotel quickly to get to the park in time as he only had minutes to spare, and the closer he got to the park, the faster his heart began to beat; it appeared that when his eyes looked at Sam, he got that same giddy feeling like he could not be happier. Finally, he was next to her, and they started to walk towards a bench next to a large oak tree with lovely green leaves hanging from its branches. They sat down and James began to think about the words he wanted to say.

"Hi Sam, it's lovely to see you! How have you been?" He leaned in and kissed her on the cheek.

"I'm great, thank you for asking! You look like you have something exciting to tell me, hope it's good news?" she was still blushing from the kiss that just happened.

"You remember that letter you gave me? Well, it said that they were very pleased in the way I acted the other day at the interviews and rehearsals, and I met up with Barbara today as she has created a male lead role doing ballet just for me." He sat there smiling as he had not finished the story and Sam quickly asked a question, "Did you take it?" She sat on the edge of her seat.

"I agreed to it and have signed a contract this morning and need to be at Town hall by seven to have a costume fitting followed by a dance rehearsal with you! I'm so excited and class myself as very lucky!" as soon as he finished speaking, Sam jumped up and hugged him tightly, as she was very happy that they were not only in a relationship but also going to be able to express their love in the form of dance, and hundreds of people would witness their love for each other.

James carried on speaking and reached for the copy of his contract he had signed, "There is only one problem, they have said I am not allowed to have any relationships with any cast member, and that would include you." Sam's face dropped to a look of seriousness as he continued speaking, "But I am not going to tell them about what we have, and how we feel about each other. I would like to propose we see each other without anyone knowing, and that way I can do what I love and see who I love without jeopardising anything. What I want you to know is nothing will ever make me leave you, as my heart just won't let me! How do you feel about this?"

Sam looked him in the eye and replied back in a softly spoken voice, "I accept what you're saying my dear, and I totally agree with what you have said, let's do it!" They hugged once more as they decided to make a move back towards their night of rehearsals and walked the long way back through the park.

The park was called 'Burnswick' and was a nice place to go to escape from what was happening in the city centre, as everything was nice and quiet inside its beautiful landscaped grounds. There was a pond that was home to the ducks and swans that were living in its waters, and seating areas were dotted around its edges, it was always rare to get a good seat to relax in this area. The grass was always well-trimmed until recently due to a number of workers that joined the army on military demand. All the trees were green and healthy; the plants were in full bloom with a mix of vibrant colours and types. All in all, the park was a peaceful place despite of the war and tough times that were going on.

As James and Sam walked through the park, they discussed what they had been up to, how they were feeling about things and how excited they were for what was ahead of them in their new roles as ballet dancers. They reached the end of the walking route that led to the main entrance of the park, by this time, they were shortly due to walk to the Town Hall for their first night.

Before they continued on, Sam looked at James again with a look of worry on her face and began to talk, "Are you ready? I think we should make our way there, don't you agree?" Her expression was still the same.

"I am if you are, my dear? Remember, as far as everyone is aware, we are just friends, and only we know the truth behind our feelings for each other!" James spoke with a serious sort of tone.

"Don't worry, we will be fine as long as we both keep our little secret! We must head there now, wouldn't want to be late!" they carried on walking towards the hotel but this time in silence.

It was rare for both of them not to talk, but James had butterflies in his stomach whilst Sam felt sick. Before they knew it, they were outside the Town Hall with only minutes to spare. They looked at each other once more.

"This is it James, our moment to rehearse and to prove ourselves has come at last," she said this quite excitedly.

"We can only do our best!" James replied.

They continued inside the building where all you could hear from the lobby was the sound of classical music and counting of what sounded like Barbara's voice saying, "One, two, three and four," repeated over, over and over again. There was a sign pinned up on the wall saying where the cast should head to once they had arrived, so they walked over to take a look. It showed that James should head to the men's room, which was to the right of the stage, and Sam to go to the women's room to the left, so they left their separate ways to meet later on when full rehearsals were to start.

James arrived at the room he was advised to go to in the lobby and was greeted by a lady with perfect curls in her hair, who was holding some clothing.

"Just on time, you must be the male dancer I was told about! James, if I understand correctly?" she said this as if she was in a rush and would accept no messing around.

"That's correct, it's nice to meet you..." James replied in a way that prompted her to reveal the details of who she was.

"Amy, I am one of Barbara's sisters. I'm in charge of design of costumes and props for the production, speaking of which, I need to take some of your measurements so I can complete the final adjustments to your costume. Do you mind if I do that now?" She looked as if it was more of a command than a request.

"Of course, that's completely fine." James stood to one side as Amy started taking his measurements, and both of them were in the room in silence, listening to what was happening outside the room. Amy finished taking the measurements and informed him that the costume would be ready within the hour, ready in time for when the first rehearsal was to start. In the other room, Sam found herself standing among 9 other successful ballet dancers, all wearing their handmade ballet costumes that looked professionally made. Barbara walked up to Sam holding her costume and told her to get changed as soon as possible, for rehearsals were to start soon. From the looks the other dancers gave her, there was something different about her costume they were not pleased about and the quiet talking between the other women confirmed this thought that Sam had.

“Go, go get changed… quickly!” Barbara said, pushing her towards the changing room. She made her way into the room and changed into her costume, and as she put it on, she changed the style of her hair and tied it into a pony tail. As she looked into the mirror, she was looking at the dress she wore, and it was beautiful. The dress was a tutu in a light cream tone with shoulder straps that were stitched at the top, holding it in place to support her figure; the bodice was tight with a tutu at the bottom that was flared out so much so that when she twirled, the costume went with her. But the part of the dress she loved most was the detail on the dress, as it had tiny balls of silver stitched to the fabric so when the light was to hit them, they would shine an effect onto anything that was around her. She stared at herself in this mirror for a long time, until she was prompted to hurry by Barbara who was shouting from another room as the women’s warm-up routine was due to begin before James was to join them. Sam replied, “Coming!” at the top of her voice to acknowledge the fact that the others were waiting for her and quickly slipped on her golden-brown ballet pumps as she started to run towards where she was required.

***

Meanwhile, James was starting to get restless and was getting nervous about how his costume was going to look, how much time he had before he had to join the women dancers, and more importantly, how well they would all dance together. He stood up when Amy came back into the room with his costume all completed and ready for him to wear.

"Here you go, James, I have done my best and it works nicely with Sam's costume. I think you will find it quite comfy too; after all, it has to be perfect otherwise I am to blame! I will wait here whilst you try it on in the back room." This was said in an uneasy sort of way.

James took the costume and went into the back room where he was prompted to change his clothes in. Once he was in his attire, he smiled as he was so excited that this would be his new character and part of his future. His costume was a pair of white tight-legged trousers that showed the outline of his legs, a blue top with some red stitching that also showed his posture very well. Over all, it was a very well-made male-style ballet suit and showed his figure perfectly. It was quite patriotic too as it followed the colours of the country's flag that everyone knew, loved and thought very highly of. He walked out of the room and turned to Amy, "It's perfect and fits well, I know people will be amazed to see all the effort you have put in, what do you think?" he said.

"I think it looks right for the part, and with you and Sam together, the look will be what the show needs. Now go, you will be late!" she said this pushing him in the direction out of the room due to Barbara's rigid schedule. She stopped him for a moment as she wanted to say one last thing before he began and hoped it would give him some confidence as she knew what the industry was like.

"Oh and James, remember no matter how much people talk or what they may whisper behind your back, only what you think matters, but more importantly, enjoy yourself. Talent like yours is hard to come by." She walked away back to her room as James smiled and continued on to his rehearsal.

He was excited and took a deep breath, and before he knew it, was taking his first step into his new role and the new him.

Chapter Five

The stage was busy with the women ballet dancers who were talking amongst themselves about how they were to look and act when the curtains fell and about how to react to certain scenes; after all, it was about war and the hope of bringing peace back to the country. It was noticeable that Sam was being cast aside by the other members as she stood in a position where the other girls had their backs to her. It was apparent that it was due to her being the lead role, she had a costume that caught the eye in certain lights and was cut in a way that it swung when she moved or went around in circles. James only noticed this as he could see jealousy in the eyes of the women talking, so he took to the stage and went straight over to Sam to greet her with the respect she deserved and acted as if they had only just met, as their agreement to keep things secret was still in place.

"Hi Sam, it's nice to see you again and may I add the costume you are wearing surely makes you stand out from the crowd, I hope people see what efforts you have put in to achieve this role!" James said this loudly so the other dancers could hear him in an attempt to ease the situation slightly.

"Why thank you, James, it's nice to be working alongside you and to meet you once more, and may I add, you look dashing too, not many people can pull off a costume like that!" she winked and smiled whilst saying this in a playful manner.

They were looking into each other's eyes and thinking about how much they wish they could be themselves, but knew this could never be, especially in a place like this. A few seconds later, everyone started to act like they were rehearsing as Barbara entered the room with a stern look on her face.

"Right everyone, I want to start tonight's practice by thanking you all for being part of this play. I could not do it without you, but I want you all to understand what I say goes. That includes you all getting along and working as a team, no excuses!" She was standing at the front of the stage with her arms crossed whilst holding a clipboard full of instructions of where she wanted people on the first scene.

"Sam and James, can you please take centre stage and go through the first scene. Remember to look graceful, and don't look down whilst dancing, on 4th count. Sam, you begin to pointe and James, you follow." Barbara started to count the beats in time with the music that was being played by Alf, the piano man.

Alf was a jolly, talkative person who was loved by many, and enjoyed the odd card game with his friends. He learnt how to play the piano 20 years ago from his father and took to the musical theatre after performing at the local drinking establishments. His face was aged and was starting to wrinkle as he liked the odd cigar or loose tobacco in his pipe, and the smell of smoke always lingered on his clothes. The clothes he wore were always the relaxed pull-over sweater and smart jeans, but would sometimes change into something more traditional at times when shows at the theatre would start. The music he was playing as James and Sam danced was a light dramatic piece by his favourite composer. He was always taken away into his own world when his fingers hit the keys, and the passion he had was noticeable.

As the music stopped, James stood in a ballet hold where it allowed him to lift Sam above his head, and as he did, Sam held her leg and body in a position that it showed the audience she was sad to see him go. The end of the scene would take the people watching to a place they all knew well at this time, a place where war had just begun and where heartbreak and hope surrounded it all.

"That was impeccably done, but you need to be more upset at your soulmate leaving, Sam and James. I need more energy with the lift at the end, let's go through it a few more times and we will bring the other dancers out for the second scene." Barbara was adamant that this should be perfect.

After a few more attempts, their moves were show-worthy, scene one was complete and the smile on Barbara's face was noticed by all. The new stage manager, Mr Charlie Coles, was wearing his denim dungarees with a bright flowery shirt underneath. He was a policeman by trade, and he had an authority look to him as his face was covered with a grey beard that was perfectly trimmed. He had a fedora hat in a grey colour that he always wore to keep his head warm no matter where he would go or end up. His shoes were black and scuffed up as these he wore all the time at work and at home, he wanted new ones but due to the war and the rations that took over he couldn't get a replacement that easily. His wife Joyce would always be close by, during the evening providing tea, coffee or cake to make sure his workforce was awarded for their hard work.

His colleagues were beginning to run backwards and forwards onto the stage with the new backdrops and props, talking between themselves of how positively they thought about scene two and how good it was going to look. Within twenty minutes, the stage looked completely different and showed a backdrop of a park and some benches were placed in front of it to give the scene a more realistic setting. It was starting to get packed full of the other ballet dancers who were told by Barbara to go on stage.

Once more they were looking at both James and Sam as if they were up to something, but this time Barbara was listening around the corner observing what was happening before she overheard one of the girls called Fiona talk out loud to the group.

"Those two think they own the place with their fancy outfits and perfect dancing. Who decided they would be right for the role? They obviously do not have any style and the ballet moves are not correct at the end" She stopped talking and looked rather worried as she noticed Barbara walk on the stage.

"I am disgusted at what you have said Fiona about your fellow dancers. How dare you speak about James and Sam like that, I took them on as lead roles together as they have the ability to dance together like it is effortless. Anything you say about them or the production is also aimed at me, as per your contract, I would like you to leave. NOW! You will not be part of this production anymore!" Barbara pointed towards the stage exit and watched as Fiona left the building still dressed in her tutu and ballet shoes.

As the door closed, Barbara began to ask, "Does anyone else have a problem with the show or crew before we carry on?"

When she finished, all of the other girls shook their heads as if they were shocked by what was going on right in front of them and began to position themselves for the second scene. This scene was to show a man beginning a journey of going to war by walking through the park, which led to the entrance of the army barracks where new soldiers were to sign up. The female dancers symbolised the family members saying their temporary farewells until a time when the war would finish. And the final act of movement would be a dramatic dance scene of James on his own, to signify his love for the family he was leaving and his fear of the unknown and whether the person he was playing would return.

They rehearsed and rehearsed this scene all evening to make sure that the pirouettes, arabesque penchés, fouettés and many others flowed into each other as if it was effortless. The moves were watched closely by Barbara, and if they were not perfect, she made each dancer repeat the move until she was satisfied. Eventually, she was happy with the results. As it was very late in the evening, she thanked everyone for the hard work they had put into the rehearsal and gave permission to go home and to come back tomorrow at the same time, except for James and Sam as she was concerned about what happened with Fiona earlier that evening.

"Are you both okay? I was a little worried that the other ballet dancers were making life difficult in the rehearsals for you," Barbara was talking with a serious tone of voice.

"We are both fine, just glad that you noticed what has been going on, each one of us are in the same boat after all," James was talking positively about it still.

Barbara ended the conversation with, "Well, I am glad and look forward to working with you both again tomorrow. Now go home and rest up and thank you once again for the hard work this evening."

Everyone left the building, leaving Mr Coles to lock up and ensure that everyone was out the building ready for the production's rehearsal time tomorrow. As they approached the front doors of the building, James and Sam heard lots of locals shouting. From the cries for help and the panic, it was clear that something was happening because of the fighter planes flying overhead, going as quickly as they could as well as the British army and wardens patrolling the streets with armed rifles ready to fire if they needed to act on suspicious behaviour.

James looked at Sam all concerned and began to talk with a worried tone, "Will you be okay going home alone, my love? Or would you like me to walk you?"

"I will be okay dear, I will see you tomorrow."

They hugged, kissed each other good bye and started their journeys home, observing the streets as the atmosphere surrounding them made them feel uneasy, but the thoughts of each other strangely made them feel at ease at the same time.

Chapter Six

James was asleep in his room at the Mesty Croft Hotel and was having a nightmare as he was reliving the events once more about the event that happened in the trench. Each time he dreamt this dream, the more graphic it would get, it became more horrific and more importantly, it made him shake with fear. The only difference this time was that he awoke in a puddle of his own sweat; it was obviously the dream as the room was cold enough you could see your own breath. He sat up and tried to compose himself, and a short while later, grabbed a drink of water from the bathroom. As he finished, he stared at himself in the mirror, trying to figure out why this was still happening.

He repeatedly said out loud, “It was only a dream, it was only a dream.” He walked back into the bedroom and turned on the radio and listened to some classical music which was quickly stopped by an urgent newsfeed from the reporter:

“Good morning to everyone listening, I am sorry to cut the music short but I have just been given the authority to report some news to you all that is very important, given to me by the UK local government. It is with much regret that the UK army have found out that there are some German soldiers who have gone missing from a holding facility in their country, and there is intelligence that they are planning on invading the United Kingdom in due course in greater numbers. This is something we believe they have taken upon themselves to do, not what they have been dictated to do. This is all we know at the moment but would ask that every single one of you remains alert and calm. However, if you do notice something that appears to be out of the ordinary, then report it to the nearest officer or soldier immediately. We thank you all and will now continue the music."

He could not believe what he just heard, it was like life and his past was haunting him together. He continued to think that his dancing was the only thing normal in his life that was keeping his mind active enough to forget about all that was happening for a long enough period of time. The time was now 14:00 hours, and he started to get his bag ready for rehearsals that evening when someone knocked on his hotel door; as he opened the door, there stood a man in a British army uniform.

Confused by the unexpected visitor, James greeted him, "Good afternoon sir, may I help you"

The soldier spoke with a voice of authority, "Hi James, the army has managed to track you down upon the advice of your mother, who said you had moved out from home and someone tracked you down as staying here. We just wanted to make sure you were safe and get a rough idea of how you are feeling now, following your discharge a while back. Are you ready to return to service? We do after all, need as much help as we can get now after the news this morning!" The soldier was looking serious as if he was going to monitor James's response.

"I am not going to be of much use to you yet sir; last night, I had another one of those flashbacks but was in a dream. I woke up in a state of terror and as much as I would like to fight for my country, I fear I will be holding everyone back rather than helping." James said this in a confident manner, in the hopes that what he said would be a good enough response.

"Ok James, that is good enough for me, we will report what you have said back to the office. Stay safe and when you feel up for joining us again, let the office know. Take care James. Oh I almost forgot, if the news this morning is true, we are going to need you either way so just bear this in mind." He closed the door behind him and left the hotel. James sighed a sigh of relief as he could not believe the morning he was having and was very careful not to say a word about the ballet show he joined knowing that soon people would find out anyway.

Time was getting on, so James packed up his things for the rehearsal that evening and headed out to the town hall. The weather was still just as cold, and the streets were empty, and no one was to be seen until he reached the front of the town hall where all the cast was waiting for Barbara to turn up with the keys to let them in. As suspected, the conversation when he arrived was about the news and also the dismissal of the dancer who was thrown off the production but talk stopped when they realised he was standing nearby. James was looking for Sam, and she was nowhere to be seen, so he began to worry as she was always one of the first to arrive, when moments later she walked around the corner with Barbara laughing and joking.

"Hi James," she shouted as they both waved.

"Sorry we are late everyone, we had a meeting about today's rehearsal and we had to give Mr Coles the chance to set up stage. I have been informed that we are ready to begin, so please get into costume and we will start in five minutes!" Barbara was excited as she was aiming to finish the production by the end of the night.

Everyone rushed into the building and began to get ready in their costumes, and as they entered the stage, the backdrop was a scene they all knew too well to date as it showed a city with rubble on the floor and buildings that looked like they had been targeted. Barbara explained to the group of ballet dancers that the next few dance scenes would show what people in the forces had to put up with but in dance form. She also told everyone how much passion she wanted to see in their expressions and movements, as this would be a vital part of the productions.

"James, the focus on these scenes would be on you as the main dancer, Hortensia and abaresque moves need to be perfect in between the other steps and positions; do you think you can do that?" Barbara said this like she was adamant it had to happen.

"It should not be a problem, as long as I can get the flow of moves to blend together, it will be fine," he said this confidently.

"Right then," she added, "all you other ballerinas need to do your pirouette turns in the background in time with each other; if one of you is out of time, then we will keep doing these scenes until you all get it. We are close to finishing the rehearsals, and I do not want this to be the reason it is delayed! Do all you girls understand?" Barbara's tone of voice was one of a strict manner, and everyone agreed and nodded their heads in silence.

James began to do the next two scenes over and over again until they were perfect, wearing a dark green top with shiny brown embroidered jewels on it with dark green tights. And the girls were lined up in the background behind him, rotating the pirouettes with Sam in the middle of the line-up. All of the girls' hair and make-up matched. Hair was victory rolled and make-up was of smart appearance including black eye shadow and bright red lipstick. Their tutus matched James's outfit, consisting of the same colours and jewels. Some of the production staff had told Barbara that the costumes were well-made and in keeping of the show, and this made her very proud indeed. Finally, there was only one scene left, one which Barbara felt the need to explain how important it was to the group as it made her cry when she wrote it. Mr Coles was pushing the last backdrop onto the stage which showed a clean town, with the British flag on bunting going across the whole stage.

"Everyone gather around, I want to explain the last scene to you before we get going," she said excitedly. "This is the last scene we are rehearsing, and it all comes down to you performing your best, and your best is all that's good enough! When I wrote this play, I wanted it to show the current events happening in the war, but also the other side which is almost forgotten. The bunting you see is because we support our families who have gone to war to fight for our country; the backdrop of the clean town is the vision of what I think will come, even if we cannot see it yet. The scene is to show everyone out there that there should be light at the end of the tunnel soon, and through the story of ballet we have created together, it should be the most touching and insightful play the people will see this year. So this part of the play will show the soldier coming back home, and James will be wearing this."

She showed a new costume which consisted of a white, blue and red jewelled top, blue tights and red ballet shoes, James took it from Barbara and went to the men's changing room and put it on. When he entered the stage area every one of the ballerinas got to their feet, and cheered and complimented him on how nice he looked.

"Now girls, it's the same James we have always had, this just proves my point of how much each and everyone one of you feels about your country. Now girls, all of you have the same costume, but as usual, Sam has a little bit different on the bodice part of her costume as she is the lead female role. The costumes are all labelled with your names, so go put them on quickly."

The tutus were a bright white colour; the bodice was blue and red with jewels placed in certain parts of the costume so that light would bounce off them when they danced, with blue pointe shoes to match. Sam's costume was the same except it had more jewels on the tutu and her pointe shoes were red to match James.

They all entered the stage area, and James whistled and applauded them all in the same way he was greeted, and as he did, smiles appeared on all the faces. They had worked as a team and they were all now supporting each other in the way that Barbara was hoping they would.

"OK everyone… places! We have an hour until closing, and if we could get it done before we go home, I will be one happy person. Please pour a 100% passion into it; you all know the moves, just make sure your moves are really emphasised when you do them. Begin!" she said this with more excitement.

The music began to flow, and it was a nice, mellow, sweet orchestra piece which showed the love and elegance of the soldier's family meeting him when he returned. After a few minutes, the music changed into an upbeat party number which made the ballet moves include lots of turns and jumps. All the ballerinas and James smiled throughout the scene, and the last bit of orchestra music got louder and louder, which led to the end of the play and final dance lift of the production. Sam ran at James who elegantly lifted her above his head whilst she held the most perfect ballet hold, at this moment Barbara and all town hall staff watching stood up and applauded all of the cast so that everyone outside could hear.

"Bravo, Bravo!!!" they all shouted.

"Thank you all so much for your hard work, and we are now set for public performances which will start on Monday. Please leave your costumes in your rooms, and we will make sure they are all ready to wear for you! Well done and see you then," Barbara said proudly.

The atmosphere was one that had been missed by all for a very long time and everyone started to leave the hall with positive feelings. James made his way back to the men's changing room to pick up his bag. On the way, he was grabbed by Sam backstage, who kissed him on the lips, not realising that there was a camera in the corner of the room that had recorded the rehearsal, and little did they know that the camera was still rolling. After congratulating each other on their performances, they got their things and left the building looking forward to the next few weeks ahead.

Chapter Seven

It was the day of the opening night of the show, and everyone was meeting at the town hall at 1:00 pm for a dress rehearsal all the way through the show. The atmosphere was one of excitement not only for the cast but also the public; there was a queue at the temporary box office for any tickets that were going spare. As each and every member went through and got tickets, they were handed a programme with a very colourful front page showing the name of the show, and inside was a brief description of the play and cast members' names, photos and roles were on the back page.

The ticket stand was put together by Mr Coles, and was a sturdy structure made of wood and had 'A British War Dance – Limited Time Only' nicely decorated in bright paint. The cast was watching this from the front doors waiting for Barbara to let them in when James noticed his mother at the front of the queue, buying some tickets and being handed the programme which she began to read whilst moving away from the queue. The door opened, and it was Barbara and she let everyone in, pointing them to the areas they needed to go to get changed, but James just stood still, watching his mother turning the pages of the programme knowing that his photo will soon be seen.

He ran over and thought in his head what to quickly say, and the words just slipped out, "Mother… what a surprise to see you here," he said out of breath. Mrs Ashfield ignored him as he continued to try and make conversation.

"It's kept my mind off things, the ballet that is, and I have met some lovely people by doing it, one in particular," James smiled pointing towards Sam.

His mother was still unhappy, as she forced some words from her mouth, "I've said it before, you will be the laughing stock of the town. If you return back in the service, they will all know, people will think differently of you."

"Look I have to go, I'm doing a dress rehearsal soon, and the manager's waiting for me. Please show the programme to your friends and come see me tonight, if you still don't like me for doing it, then you are obviously not as supportive as I once thought. Enjoy the show Mother… if you can be bothered!" he looked at his mom with a serious look, a look that his brother had never seen before when he was alive and that was saying something as he had always been the serious type.

James walked indoors to get ready for the dress rehearsals, and when he turned around and looked behind him, he saw his mother staring back at him, looking all confused about what had just happened. James noticed she was walking away to go home holding tickets in her hands, and he thought she was finally coming around to the idea that he was a ballet dancer.

Inside the town hall, the room was full of red padded chairs and the stage was all set for the evening production. The stage was shiny, as it had been cleaned and the oak bounced the light that was shining on it from the lighting rigs that had been put up. There were new curtains installed, posh red cotton tied together at the sides to make it look like a proper theatre setting. The backdrops had been positioned and placed on wheels, so they could be pushed on and off stage in between scenes and from the ceiling hung some cardboard cut-outs of spitfires that had been made by the local art community especially for the play. In front of the stage, the orchestra was beginning to set up, a local group that had learnt music provided to them by Barbara, as she wanted it to be as perfect as possible. Everyone was ready, and the orchestra began the music, the ballet dancers were instructed to perfect the moves they felt needed more attention and the dress rehearsal began.

Scene by scene, again and again, they went over the production until it was perfect for the evening performance. Finally, Barbara was happy and shouted out instructions so everyone could hear. "Well done everyone! You may all go to the restroom to begin getting ready for tonight's performance, except for you two, James and Sam, I want to have a word with you about something." Everyone left but the two told to wait, looking at each other, not knowing if she knew about their secret relationship.

"Are you aware that my show is in your hands tonight, and are you two sure you have the emotion in you to get my message across to the paying public, the one we spoke about yesterday?" James and Sam nodded as a response.

"And finally is there anything you would like to tell me that I should know?" She looked at them like she knew something and they responded by shaking their heads sideways, as they felt it was the safest way without giving anything away.

"Ok my dears, go join the others, we have a show to put on!" she smiled and walked away to make sure all the other staff were doing the final preparations.

It was time, the crowds gathered outside the front doors of the town hall, the sky was dark with stars that were shining brightly and the air was cold with a fine mist that could be seen in the distance. Everyone had on their shoulders emergency bags, which carried supplies such as gas masks in case of a raid during a performance, and everyone was wearing their smartest clothing as night outs were classed as a novelty during these hard and challenging times happening around them.

Inside, the cast could hear the hustle and bustle from everyone waiting to enter and sit in their allocated seats. They soon heard the announcement that the doors were now open, and people were to get refreshments and take their seats as the show was to begin in 30 minutes. Before the double doors on the entrance to the main hall stood a young 20-year-old boy, who was wearing a dinner suit with a tray around his neck selling drinks and snacks as he greeted everyone entering the room. He was very skinny and his skin was perfect and lightly toned with a voice so deep he appeared to be older than he was to people who met him.

Moments later, Mrs Ashfield entered the building, wearing a light yellow dress, seamed stockings and mustard coloured high heels to match. Mrs Ashfield asked the man to show her to the seat she had booked, and she was soon in the main hall a few rows back from the stage. An announcement was made that the show was about to begin, and everyone was welcomed to the show.

The orchestra started the opening music and talking around the room faded away as the hall lights were turned off. The lighting rig shined onto the closed red curtain, the music got more and more dramatic when suddenly Barbara pulled the curtains' cord and as they opened, they were tied to the side by two of the stage production team. One by one, the ballet dancers entered the stage and performed the first scene. The acting and ballet combined had guests glued to their seats watching with much anticipation, and as James entered the stage, everyone was shocked at the fact that there was a male dancer in the production, and some started to look at the programme to find out more about him.

Mrs Ashfield acted as if she didn't know who it was and just sat their smiling, pretending she was happy. The show got to halfway point and an interval was announced, and before she knew it, the second part had started once again. She watched as the ballerinas danced through the last of the scenes which led to the part of James lifting Sam in the air. As he lifted her, the whole hall stood up to applaud, every cast member included. And to James's disbelief, even Mrs Ashfield was among them. As people took their bows, Mrs Ashfield was now telling everyone around her that the male dancer was her son and how proud she was of him. People started to leave the hall and Mrs Ashfield sat back in her seat waiting for James to be dismissed to go home and was approached by Barbara.

“Thank you for coming, but may I ask you to retire from the building as we need to clean the hall ready for tomorrow’s performance. We do hope you enjoyed the show,” she looked at her as if she wanted Mrs Ashfield to leave straightaway.

“I had a wonderful time, the message you portrayed is one that all of us can relate to and it was lovely to see my son James perform, that’s why I am waiting around you see… so I can congratulate him.” Mrs Ashfield said happily.

“Oh well your son is one to defiantly be proud of, let me see if he is ready; he should be ready to leave any moment as he will need his rest for tomorrow,” Barbara smiled and walked away.

She walked backstage and found James and Sam alone in one of the meeting rooms kissing and began to speak in an upset tone.

“I don’t have to tell you how angry I am to see you both acting like this, and if it wasn’t for my play, you would both be fired from the show… think yourselves lucky; I’m not going to dismiss you… James, your mother is waiting for you in the main hall, see you both tomorrow.” As she walked away, both of them could tell how angry she was and decided to go home.

James picked up his belongings off the floor and proceeded to go and see his mother who he could see as he looked across the stage. As he approached, his mother hugged him tightly and she began to speak, “I am so sorry, Son, and I am so proud of your performance. I never knew you could do ballet that well! How did you learn it?” she asked with excitement.

James looked at his mother’s expression before he began to speak, “Well, I started learning when I was a young boy, whenever there was music I would practice the movements and dance moves from anything I could copy them from. I hid in my room, embarrassed by what people may think about me and now look, I'm the lead in a ballet production. Thomas knew about it too but he didn't take too kindly to it at first as he was worried what people in the army might think, but it keeps my mind active, at night the nightmares of what happened on the battlefield flow constantly, and this is the only thing that has saved me. If it wasn't for this, I would eventually have had to make the choice to either seek further help or end it for myself.

"Ballet is my life now mother, and all I am asking is that you accept it. I have met someone too and I would like you to meet her soon. Her name is Sam, you will know her already as the main female ballerina you have seen tonight. I will introduce you to her personally soon, but for now, we need some rest." He smiled at her to comfort his mother from what she had just been told.

"I will always support you, Son, especially now, and any choices you make I will always help with, no matter what!" she hugged him one last time.

It was Monday of the third week of December, and the city of Birmingham was in a festive spirit. In the windows of houses stood Christmas trees decorated with lights and decorations and the front doors had wreaths hanging on them. The streets were full of cheer, and carol singers were spreading joy through the neighbourhood.

The cast continued to do daily showings of the show and on Saturdays would do a matinee show so people who worked long hours could attend too. The papers started to write good reviews and articles were starting to circulate around the country and even hit the London theatre district. Every evening was packed and each performance sold out, Barbara never thought that her ballet show would be such a success. Barbara was at the town hall and decided to give the cast a small party before the night's performance and brought in her radio from home.

All they could find was news on the radio so everyone listened, waiting for the music to start which stated the following by a serious spokesman:

"The government has been given an official statement and have said that it is only fair that the British public must know. There have been some reports of some German army troops entering our country, and it is much sadness to say that they have succeeded. We have been provided with some intelligence that they are said to be hiding around the Birmingham area. We have therefore increased security and deployed more troops in the district to patrol the streets and ask that anyone who lives in Birmingham to be alert and stay safe. If you notice anything strange, please report it to the nearest officer, soldier or warden immediately. We would all like to wish you a merry Christmas and hope for a positive new year for us all. Thank you for listening." The news finished and music started and the cast sat there quietly thinking about what had just been said.

"Come on everybody, let's make the most of the time we have together and here's to another show this evening!" Barbara raised a glass and the party and the show continued as normal.

Chapter Eight

Once again, the sky was filled with nothing but a black blanket and a cold layer of mist. The streets were quite empty, there was a moment of silence which made the roads a place of fear and uncertainty of what may happen soon due to the radio announcements and headlines in the newspaper. Only one thing was sure, Birmingham was on high alert and all residents were told to prepare themselves for the uncertain times ahead, ensuring that they are ready to make the most difficult of sacrifices if ordered to do so, even if it meant the most to them, as Birmingham was now at war and public safety was key.

It was a Thursday afternoon, the town clock hit 16:00 hours, and on the radio, an important news story was being read out slowly, by a man with a deep voice that had a sense of worry and urgency to it:

"We have been informed by our forces that are patrolling our streets, who are doing a grand job may I add, that there have been reports of the enemy planning to invade our city this evening, in the hunt for a man named James. We have some idea who this may be and we ask that person to stay alert at all times. We will however not name him on national radio, but I must ask him to think about his options of what is right and wrong, either way, we support him." This man took a deep breath, and started to sound upset even though his speech continued to be strong:

"I am now going to give you all some instructions which must be followed through, it is as upsetting for me to ask this of you all in this hour of need but it will keep your families safe until this war is over. All families in the Birmingham area must pack their children a small bag or suitcase containing only the essentials such as clothing, labelling it clearly with the name of your children as they will be evacuated out of the city centre by 18:00 hours tonight. The location to take them to will be Birmingham Train station where your children will be allocated another family to live with on the outskirts until further notice. Please be assured that your children will be well looked after and will return home when it is safe to do so. Thank you all and sorry for any upset this has caused you all."

The speech went on in more detail including what to do if an air raid siren sounded during the evacuation, if anyone knocked your door, not to answer it even if you are expecting somebody, and more importantly, they must still try and lead as close to a normal life as possible.

The streets started to become so busy it was like being in a whole new world; mothers and fathers were running with their children, all gossiping and quickly moving along the streets gripping their hands tightly with one hand and carrying the small cases of clothes and belongings with the other. The younger of the children were questioning the parents as to why this was happening, although no information was being given to them. The younger children who were being dragged around by their parents were mostly being carried on their parents' shoulders, whilst the faces all housed a look of sadness. Children's eyes were filled with tears from the thoughts of never seeing their parents again or even if they would see their families at all.

The time was close to 17:30 hours, and Birmingham Train Station was so busy, a queue of people led into the street next to it. Police and army personnel were making sure the flow of people panicking was moving as quickly as possible. They noticed a small boy by the name of Frederick crying in the corner of the station as other people just walked by without even asking if he was okay. As the policeman walked up to Frederick, he took a few steps backwards, and the policeman began to speak, "Are you okay, young Sir? What's your name?" the policeman smiled to ease the situation for the boy.

"My name's Frederick! Am I in trouble?" the boy asked this whilst drying the tears from his eyes onto his dirty shirt.

"No not at all, where are your parents?" a smile appeared on the policeman's face to try and comfort the young boy.

"We were told we had to go on a train, and my sister Hannah started playing up and we all lost each other. Mother told us we are having a trip away together, just me and my sister, staying with friends. I've never seen, met or heard of them in Mother and Father's conversations before either." Frederick was so confident at this point but started biting the bottom of his lip wondering if he had said more than he should have done.

The policeman took further details from Frederick, held his hand and started to walk through the crowds, whilst he said, "I know just where they will be, stay close to me and I will take you back to your parents."

Along the way, Frederick was looking at the policeman's uniform that seemed to fit loosely around his body. The jacket was made of a thick black wool, and the trousers were being held up by light grey braces and a leather belt with a brass buckle that shined in light as they walked through the station. His boots were clean and made from the highest quality leather that had been issued by the forces. As they approached the second platform of the station, Frederick was starting to ask more and more questions and suddenly stopped for a moment.

"Thank you for your help, Sir! May I ask what your name is?" Frederick stood staring at the policeman waiting for an answer, as they were near the platform.

"Constable Stevens is my name, Frederick. Let us go find your parents now, shall we?" They smiled at each other and began walking down the wooden stairs of the bridge, where Frederick's parents stood with Hannah in their arms looking all worried.

Constable Stevens started to walk away quickly back to the entrance of the station whilst Frederick's family joined the crowd waiting for the announcement, but then walked back to say one last thing to Frederick, "You are a bright, young lad Frederick, you take care of yourself."

Turning to his parents, he added, "By the way, do not move anywhere, Miss Salmon is about to announce more about your children's trip but for now enjoy the scenery of the station." He smiled and walked away quickly.

The station was a lovely building, the front of the building was built with red bricks and over the top lay green and cream coloured wood which made it look like it had an upper-class standard. There was a glass window, centred neatly at the front of the building with a serving hatch at the bottom for Bianca the ticket lady to pass people's passes through during busy hours. Inside the station were only two platforms which were accessible over a white wooden-painted bridge that had a black cast-iron clock on the side of it. The roof was held up by iron pillars and was covered in spider webs, and the ceiling was painted with a display of flowers which had been there since the late 1800s. One thing that stood out most of all, was a little stage where a wooden grand piano sat for passengers to play whatever came to mind.

As everyone stood patiently in the station waiting for further instructions, Miss Salmon's voice finally made an appearance on the station's microphone. Miss Salmon was a high-class lady who had experience of working in a background of jobs from well-established businesses which included her organising their workload. With her reputation in mind, the local government contacted her to arrange the evacuation of the children from Birmingham to countryside locations. Miss Salmon had dark red hair that was neatly styled with two victory rolls, and she wore subtle make-up so her bright red lips stood out more than anything else she had put on her face that day. Her clothing consisted of a two-piece suit which was chocolate brown in colour with a white, clean, perfectly ironed blouse under the jacket and if people looked closely, they would notice her initial S sewn neatly into it. Her shoes were a light brown too with a strap that buckled over the top of her feet; Miss Salmon always looked elegant no matter what she wore. Her expertise and glamour made her one of the well-known members of the community. The crowds of children with their families were now standing quietly as the announcement began.

"I would like to thank every one of you for acting so promptly following the news of the events that are said to follow shortly. Your government understands that it is hard letting go of the things that mean so much to you, especially when it comes to the ones you love dearly. I would firstly like to point out that your children have all been allocated a place to live in the countryside until the recent or upcoming events have passed, and we have given strict guidelines to all those involved. The safety of your children is key, and the government would like to reassure you all that the choices made have been done so in confidence." She took a deep breath and continued.

"You have all been allocated a tag for your child which corresponds with the carriage they must board. As time is quickly passing us, you have five minutes to say your farewells as we must depart the trains immediately due to the tight schedule we have in place. Thank you one and all for your co-operation, and we hope you understand our government's actions, we hope to reunite you all soon with priority." Miss Salmon turned off her microphone and watched the most difficult thing she has ever had to do.

With the sound of families saying their goodbyes, the atmosphere was filled once more with tears of sadness around the station, but more importantly, with love. Station staff was starting to load the carriages of the train with the luggage and belongings, and the children started to board the train, embarking on their journey without the loved ones they knew. Few of the children had to be pulled away from their parents as they couldn't bear a life without them. The trains were filled with children and luggage, and steam started to rise from the chimney at the engine room, the driver pulled on the red cord and the noise from the horn filled the station with a deep tone, and the trains slowly pulled off into the distance. All that was left was silence, tissues and hankies were waved as parents said final goodbyes… for now. Miss Salmon made her final announcement in a more softly spoken tone as she turned the station microphone back on:

"Thank you all, and once again we know how hard this has been for all involved. We would like to ask to return to your homes as quickly as possible as the night is drawing near and your safety is too imperative to us." Once more, the microphone turned off and she left the station, driving away in her car.

Everyone else started to leave the station quickly and were being escorted back into Birmingham as the city was still on high alert. As they approached the town, all the houses had been allocated sandbags which leant against the walls, street lamps were covered in posters that had been stuck up by the council. People were still going about their daily activities, living like nothing was happening. Some people were going home, some going to the local shops and the evening visitors going to the ballet show that was still scheduled to go ahead that evening.

Inside the town hall, the chairs and stage were set for the evening performance, and Barbara was ensuring all the costumes had been placed in the dressing rooms ready for curtain call. A short while later, James and Sam walked through the door, preparing for the meeting that was scheduled to discuss the news that was announced on the radio. All the ballerinas were sitting in the room in a circle, not speaking a word to each other as they were all deep in thought, in the corner stood Barbara smiling nervously. As James and Sam took to their seats, Barbara began to speak, "Thank you all for coming to the hall early tonight, you are all aware that tomorrow is the last show. Due to the news and unfortunate events that may occur, we all need to prepare ourselves for any situation." Barbara pointed to a wall.

Everyone was now looking at a map of the town hall, and Barbara pointed out all the exits, old and new, and all other security measures she had put in places which included hidden compartments and hideaways. She continued to speak, "I am grateful for everything, what each and every one of you has done for my production and you are all very talented people. Enjoy your last two nights of performing, and let's give our audience something to remember!" Barbara left the room and everyone headed for their dressing rooms to get ready for the evening show.

As the room started to empty, the air raid sirens started once more and outside the panic struck the town. The German army that everyone knew so much about had entered the city, and the firing of guns sounded through the sky whilst the shouting of orders between members of the British army were easily heard. In the distance, the screams of people who lived in Birmingham could be heard in the distance which sent spine-tingling shivers down everyone's back.

A meeting was being held with a group of British army leaders who had been telegrammed some information that there were now two German armys, and the one they were fighting against was not who you think it was. This army was after one person and one person only, and anyone in the way was going to get hurt regardless; they were after James. On the report, it stated that this second army had a group of ten troops and had similar suits, which were grey in colour with black webbing, a symbol on the sleeves was translated to 'it marks the end'. The army had at this point, already entered the city and had run passed the town hall into the busiest area they could find, with one task on their minds… finding out more on James's whereabouts.

They grabbed everyone they could find, men, women, wardens, and they would not give up until they were satisfied that the person they were talking to knew nothing about James, or could at least help them. Anyone they found suspicious was held hostage in a camouflaged lorry they had disguised as a British vehicle. The lorry was green and had netting on top with dark and light leaves to make it look like it had been used for a long time. There were currently seven people held in the back, all fearing for their lives. The only thing keeping them going was the distinct sounds of British fighter planes in the sky, searching for potential oppositions and keeping the skies clear.

The leader of this army made his way back to the vehicle and in his German language asked his army if they had asked everyone if they knew of James and that he would not rest until he had carried out his deed as James had killed his brother. His army advised him they had done their best, but some people were missing from houses and some of the shops, so answers he wanted were still possibly out there hiding.

Not realising what was happening, Mrs Ashfield, walked straight past the lorry thinking it was one of the British army. She was noticed by one of the troops and got pushed up against the side of the lorry with a gun pointing to her head.

"Do not worry old lady, you tell me what I want, you do not get hurt," his German accent was thick and strong saying the little English he knew. "Where is James Ashfield? Do you know him or where he may be?" he looked at her as he spoke closely next to her face

Mrs Ashfield's heart began to beat fast and her hands started to shake. The thought of telling this man the truth was too much for her to handle, and she started to think of the quickest lie she could come up with. A lie which would save the life of one of her son, her own flesh and blood, and before she knew it, she began to speak whilst his hands were tightly around her neck.

"I have never heard or seen of this man you speak of in my life before, who is he?" She said this with certainty so his grip would loosen and as it did, the German soldier ordered his troops to start the lorry. Mrs Ashfield carried on her statement, "I have however heard a rumour that he has moved on to the next town in the hope of avoiding anything that may happen during this awful time you are in control of. Now let me go, I'm not the one you want!"

He let go of her and pushed her onto the ground which was full of dirt and broken items that had been destroyed during the war. The second army jumped into the lorry and the wheels started to spin, creating a cloud of dust as they sped off into the distance, hoping the information Mrs Ashfield had given them was the truth. This German army was on a mission to the end and the talking between them must have been coded as no one would understand them, even if they knew the language they spoke.

They arrived in the next town of Walsall, which to look at was in the same state as Birmingham, except there were more bombed out areas and sites of destruction. The same procedure was carried out by the leader of the army and they continued to ask everyone about James and his location, which went on for hours and hours until eventually they gave up. Each of them climbing back into the lorry until one of them realised a poster with the letters J and A next to each other, ripping the address off the poster they made their way to the address, the address was to the ballet show. This was the answer they were looking for, something that would lead them straight to James, with a smile they travelled as quickly as they could back to Birmingham with their objective in mind.

Chapter Nine

The city of Birmingham was going through its highest rate of security measures ever put in place in its history. All military personnel were still looking for possible signs of movement that were deemed as suspicious, and all reports, telegrams or correspondence were being monitored by a team of four. The streets were paved with constant reminders of the tragedy that was happening before everyone's eyes and the destruction that has happened in the past and forthcoming events. Members of the community were at their homes or places of safety in working environments.

It was late afternoon and people started to emerge from homes, shops and began to leave for work, as the city seemed to become a safer place, well it felt that way anyway. All police, army, service men and women continued to patrol the streets and had been ordered by the local government to increase protection at the main entrances in and out of Birmingham. It was a cold day with clear skies ahead and the low winds gave an impression of calm evening ahead. Shops remained open to gather as much business as possible to the town they loved. The town hall started to get busy at 17:00 hours, as people were determined to carry on as normal of a life as they possibly could and wanted to treat themselves to a ballet performance. Tonight was the last night of the production and the ballerinas were starting to arrive for another meeting and final rehearsal.

Barbara was standing in front of a row of chairs that had been set up and smiled at everyone as they took to their seats. The look of fear, concern and excitement was all rolled into one, on every one of the ballerinas' faces. James and Sam sat next to each other with their shoulders touching, after all this was as close as they could get to each other inside the town hall. It was so difficult for both of them not being able to show their love towards one another, as the other ballerinas still did not know of the relationship they had. Once everyone was settled and seated, Barbara did her best to keep a normal, upbeat attitude but inside she was feeling very anxious and scared. Barbara could not wait much longer as she looked at everyone sitting around her, took a deep breath and said her last speech of words and encouragement; she started to speak in her friendly and confident manner.

"Well… the day has come when our show must end. Since day one of this production, each one of you has danced the best of ballets to the best of your abilities, and I am very proud. Your ballet movements and confidence have portrayed a story in which I cannot fault. So, thank you, to each and every one of you for your efforts. Tonight is our last performance, and I would like to see us all make it one to remember. I have, however, been asked to inform you that the city of Birmingham is in a state of high alert and the threats from the enemy is still very much active. I therefore ask, if an air raid siren sounds, we will cease performing until the all-clear is given. I hope you all enjoy your last night performing and once again thank you!" Barbara finished her speech as a tear fell slowly down her cheek and she left the room.

All the ballerinas started to discuss different topics from the war to how upset they were that this was going to be there last performance. One of the girls kept staring every now and then at James and Sam because she knew something was not quite right with the way they had been behaving. After 20 minutes of non-stop gossip and conversations, the ballerinas all picked up their shoes and started to walk to the dressing rooms one last time. James and Sam were the only ones left in the meeting room and went to kiss each other on the lips. As they did, Catrina walked in on them and in a state of shock picked up her ballet pumps she had forgotten on her way out and ran out of the room, in denial of what she had just seen as this could ruin the reputation of the production if she was to say anything.

Looking all worried after just being caught out, Sam turned to James, "What we going to do? Barbara will be so mad if she was to find out we have been seeing each other!" her face was a fiery red in colour.

"My dear, I will take the blame if anything was to happen, after all tonight is our last performance. What is the worst that could happen?" James picked up his bag, kissed Sam on the forehead and headed to his room. As he left, Sam blushed and sat in the corner of the room, thinking about how happy this production had made her, especially James.

It was now an hour left for the beginning of the first act and the theatre started to become a busy and loaded place, full of excited and happy visitors. The town hall was in full swing, Barbara had prepared a piano in the entrance which had her husband playing classical music for her younger class of girls who were aged between nine and thirteen years, performing a ballet routine for guests as they entered the building. Standing by the theatre door was a barman in an evening suit serving glasses of cheap champagne, as she had managed to get extra rations from the local shop on the corner of the same street. Guests took to their seats in the theatre, men were wearing black evening suits and the women wore their best cocktail dresses or suits with matching hats and fascinators. The lights faded down, marked the start of show time. As the lights faded, so did the voices in the audience, then the curtains rolled up.

Act one began and onto the stage went the first of ballerinas led by Catrina, doing a sequence of three different moves, consistently flowing elegantly into each other. The ballet scene represented a mother and her daughters saying good bye to their relatives who had joined the army and had been summoned to leave for war.

As the music changed to move on to its next act, stage staff moved the next backdrop onto the stage, which included an imitation of a battlefield. At the front of the stage was a piece of wood which had barbed wire painted onto it and hanging from the ceiling were again pieces of wood but cut and painted into the shape of bomber planes and spit fires. The music was now of a deep tone, and James entered to do his solo ballet number; he pirouetted, turned, leaped in a timely fashion, owning the stage as he did so. This routine showed how he felt when he was in the war and was made so much easier for him to perform because of his own experiences. On his last pirouette, Sam made her appearance onto the stage and as she did, they performed a move together that involved Sam being held above his head. They held the move perfectly still for around ten seconds whilst the classical piano music changed into a calming sound.

Act Three was now on its way which was a time for Sam and James to be passionate with their moves, making sure it was a scene of love. Barbara had written this scene to show an army soldier falling in love with a lady who worked within the royal air force. On stage, a background consisting of a field and a lake was pushed on by the production staff, and Sam began to do her ballet routine whilst she incorporated moves that would support her when lifting and turns were involved. The looks on the faces of the audience were smiling whilst eyes were fixed on James and Sam. They were near the end of the scene and James was currently holding Sam in a ballet move called a 'Fish Dive'.

Suddenly, the air raid siren began to sound and the doors to the theatre swung open. Standing in the doorway were four men from the German army holding guns in their hands that everyone had been warned about. The leader was Wilhelm, seeking revenge on James for what had happened in Germany.

"We are looking for James Ashfield, and no one is leaving here until we have him, we know he is here as we have this!" Wilhelm was holding the poster he had found in Walsall. "Now where is he?" his accent had become thicker as time went by.

He walked down the aisle of one row and picked on a woman in the audience who screamed as she pointed to the stage. The four men began to run towards to the stage, pushing over anyone who tried to stop him, until eventually they were on the stage. James and Sam had already run in their ballet pumps to the back exit which was accessed via a hatch at the back of the stage and were running as quickly as they could towards to the front of the building. Little did they know, the Germans were waiting for them there too.

As they both approached the front of the town hall, they got caught by the two German soldiers who pushed them both against the wall, holding guns to the chest of James and forcefully holding Sam so she couldn't move. Sam was in tears, shouting, "Please don't!" from the top of her voice, the only thing James wanted was for Sam to be safe, but it was too late. During the struggle of trying to help one another, the sound of a gunshot was heard through the door way; it was Wilhelm, and Sam fell to floor hitting her head as she did.

"Stop!" The voice was coming from across the way, followed by several warning shots. It was a group of the British army and a medical officer which had been patrolling the streets that evening. As they approached, the German army were being chased by military vehicles with gun fires and loud bangs that followed. James was kneeling on the floor, his hands covered in Sam's blood as he tried to stop the wound from losing any more, as the more he tried to keep her attention, the weaker she got.

"Stay with me," he said, "Don't you leave me on my own!" He took a deep breath as he continued, "You do know everything I have done since we have met has been for you? You walked into my life and gave it meaning… belonging, please stay with me, don't let go, please! Please!" Tears were dripping to the ground as his head fell to meet his chest.

In between the pain, she was experiencing, Sam put on a brave smile and said, "My darling, you have given me everything I have ever wanted, but it is my time to let go. I will go up to the heavens and when you see rain, it means I am doing our ballet routine on the clouds, and my…" She stopped suddenly and gasped for air before continuing, "my dying wish is to see you perform our routine one more time, promise me, I will… I will see you one last time." She was struggling to keep her eyes open.

James turned to the medical officer and asked him to help carry her back into the theatre so he could keep her final promise, James held her feet whilst the officer picked her up by the shoulders and started to make their way to the front. The audience were staring at James's costume covered in blood and were in shock when they noticed Sam being assisted by a medical officer. Barbara came over and hugged James as he told her he didn't have time to explain but told her the music he wanted to be played.

In a choked up voice, Barbara instructed the pianist to play Sam's favourite classical music which she practiced ballet to as a child. Step by step, James performed the most perfectly put together routine he made up as a present he was going to give her after the show was over. His pointes, turns, leaps all flowed once more beautifully into one another, he was positioned on the stage in front of Sam the whole way through and as he finished the final move, he heard the last words Sam would ever say in a faint voice, "I love you!" Her eyes closed and arm fell. The audience was silenced, and James sat on the edge of the stage with a broken heart, which he knew could never be fixed. He composed himself, and said his final words to her whilst holding her hand, "I will fight for you and I will see you in heaven." Kissing her forehead one last time, he was then asked to leave the premises with Barbara and the other ballerinas, by an army officer who was given orders to clear the site.

Chapter Ten

It was the day after the terrible event that had happened, and Birmingham was in a state of shock and denial. Outside of the town hall, people were giving tributes of love, friendship, respect and the community were placing flowers on the cold cobbled street to show they were thinking of James but more importantly in memory of Sam. It showed a sign that when a war is happening around the world, a little bit of hope can be given to the people who feel as if all is lost and they are alone.

Inside the town hall, James sat quietly, deep in thought. His head was resting on his hands; his eyes were filled with a pool of tears that ran down his cheek and slowly into the corner of his mouth where it met the sound of sadness. He was struggling to breath and his heart was broken, for it was something love could no longer conquer, after being torn into irreparable pieces. James just wanted to be alone.

The walls of the hall were destroyed by gun fire, leaving holes in the fabric of the building, with rubble on the floor beneath it. Wooden furniture was broken and destroyed, not resembling what it once was, and all that was left intact was the stage with its background still standing proudly behind it as a reminder of the last dance James and Sam did together. The wall to the left of the stage only had the bottom half remaining with the top half on the floor surrounding it, and the other wall to the right still had its stain glassed window with not a break in it.

James had been sitting for hours and had thought about many things, how much he loved Sam, the day he saved her from messing up her opportunity to audition, but what he could not stop thinking of most of all was the way she passed away. The images were embedded in his mind, the worst sort of images that he couldn't erase from his memory. He thought of ballet to try and forget about the recent events that have happened and he began to smile. He was picturing the routine they performed together every night, how pretty Sam looked in her sparkling tutu, costumes and how they made each other smile.

"Right!" he shouted.

He decided he was going to make her proud and do what she would have wanted him to. He picked up his ballet shoes that he had hung on the back of his chair and started to walk over the rubble and broken glass that lay on the floor, jumping onto the stage, taking the centre position and began pirouetting. As he did, taking breaks so that he could move into a different position, again every move was done precisely. James didn't like making errors when it came to ballet and performances and beads of sweat dripped from his face until he finished his practice with a dramatic ending. James took a break sitting on the edge of the stage, taking deep breaths whilst deciding what he should do. A few moments later, he remembered he had a photo of himself and Sam before the opening night of them dressed up in performance costumes. He pulled the picture from his briefcase which was initialled with his and Sam's names on it. The case was a light brown in colour with brass locks that held the lid down securely. He stared at the picture for a while before jumping to his feet, running into the changing rooms.

Hanging up in the women's changing room was Sam's costume and tutu all covered in her blood from the night before. Opening the case, he placed her costume and tutu inside along with her ballet pumps. He also found a diary that she had been keeping, not wanting to know what she would have written he thought it was best he should keep this with him too before other people disturbed her privacy. He continued to his own dressing room and placed his own costume, tights and shoes into the case on top of the stuff that belonged to Sam.

Once again, his thoughts were running wild about Sam and decided he was going to make her proud, and proud is what she would have been. Grabbing his overcoat off the coat hook, he ran to the front of the building and was on his way to see Barbara one last time. James knew that if he had the chance of finding Barbara he would need to speak with the other ballerinas that were part of the show; after all, everyone was in hiding after what happened the night before. He searched for hours and hours upon end for the ballerinas he did not get to know, the only one that made any sort of interaction was Catrina. Deciding to take a break, he headed down a quiet road called Oxford Street.

The road was short with detached houses, with blocks of flats that separated them, all allowing accommodation for up to 30 families. The walls of every building, including windows, had a thick layer of dirt made by industrial pollution from the factories that stood at the back of each row, not to mention the dust from the bombed-out houses during the war.

James sat at the curb and opened his brown case, once again being reminded by the death of his recent love, he pulled out the diary that belonged to Sam. Holding this diary in his hand, James felt uneasy about reading someone's personal life, thoughts and feelings, but if anyone was going to have Barbara's address, it would have been Sam. Opening the front cover slowly, he was greeted with pages upon pages of writing, but he had no time to find out these details and started to flick through the pages until he came across the telephone numbers which were not linked to any names and an address section. Within it there was nothing for Barbara, but strangely saw the ballerina's address called Catrina, Sam got friendly with her towards the end of the production. His next option was to visit Catrina, shutting his case and jumping to his feet, he made the next part of his journey to get more information.

Ten minutes later, he arrived at number 15 Peters Street, a calm and quiet area where buildings were neatly built standing proudly next to each other. Number 15 was built with a mixture of brown and grey bricks with matching roof tiles. The garden lawn was overgrown but the edges of the lawn were filled with bright-coloured plants and flowers. As James approached the front door, he noticed something odd, the door was slightly open and his body became anxious that somebody may be inside or worse still, something could have happened to Catrina too.

James opened the door fully and knocked three times, shouting "Catrina!" each time he did so, but no one replied. Becoming worried, he rushed through the rooms of the house one by one, looking all around him as he did, until he reached the bathroom. Sitting on the edge of the bathtub was Catrina crying continuously whilst her hands were shaking at the same time. James kneeled on the floor in front of her, and as he did, Catrina fell into his arms.

"Catrina, what has happened? Are you okay?" James spoke to her really concerned.

"They came, the men who killed Sam, they followed me home. They tortured me until I told them everything I knew about you and where you may be, then they left. They are after you, James, please give yourself up or pray to the gods above for help. Many more people may be at risk, and they have gone to Barbara's house, please can you go and make sure she is safe and well?" Catrina spoke so quickly as she was very upset.

James knew what he must do but needed further details on where Barbara lived, turning to Catrina he asked, "Can you please tell me where Barbara is, Catrina, that is why I came here, and now I am glad I did because I now know that you are not in danger too!"

James started to smile at Catrina, holding out his hand as she passed him a piece of paper that had the address he needed written in a very fancy handwriting.

"I want you to know that none of this was meant to happen and from the bottom of my heart, I am sorry you have been included in this awful war, God bless you Catrina!"

James left the property, closing all the doors behind him, stepping back onto the street, unfolding the piece of paper he was just given. There was Barbara's address:

62 Sycamore Avenue, Birmingham.

Folding the paper back together, James started to run as quickly as he could, checking his watch as he knew time-keeping, especially today, was very important. The more he ran, the more he wanted to succeed, even though his body just wanted to rest, he knew that this was not an option. Twenty minutes had passed, and he finally arrived at Sycamore Avenue, one of the posher areas of Birmingham. He paused and studied the doors carefully, looking for the number where Barbara lived, until he finally reached the gated area.

He opened the wooden gate and it made a squeaking noise as it closed behind him, and he walked down the slabbed garden path. In front of the glass windowed, oak wooden door was a welcome mat with a sign next to it, instructing people to wipe their feet before entering the house, after all everyone knew Barbara hated the thought of somewhere being dirty. On the door hung a heavy iron door knocker, James banged it three times as loudly as he could with no answer. Once again, he started to become worried and looked under the welcome mat to find an envelope labelled with his name on it. Carefully opening it, he pulled out a piece of paper which read,

'James, enter the house via the side alley where you will find a wooden door, which will lead you to the back of my house. Enter my house via that door.'

Barbara knew he would need her at some point in the next few days following Sam's death and carefully planned this note for when he needed her the most. As he approached the back door, he opened it to find the house was in silence, each room following on to another in the same way.

Barbara's house was decorated with floral wallpaper that consisted of many pastel colours that blended nicely into one another, with its furnishings matching to the highest of standards that were made from the best wood or fabric. As James was moving through the dining room, in the corner stood a large glass cabinet being held upright by carved, twisted wooden legs supporting its weight. Inside was a display of pictures of all the shows she had promoted, produced or simply put routines together for at the theatre. Medals upon medals and pictures upon pictures of her work stood proudly next to each other; in the centre of the cabinet, James noticed a photograph of himself and Sam performing a ballet-lift in a wooden photo frame. He took it out of the cabinet carefully, and took a few moments to remember Sam for who she was before placing it back into its centre spot as everything seemed to be placed in a particular way.

He heard rustling coming from up the stairs, so he began to climb the dark wooden staircase, each step creaking as he put his weight onto it. Finally reaching the landing, he noticed three different doors with brass handles. The door in front was wide open, so James opened the door next to it, which was the pink and cream bathroom, no one was in there. Knowing that someone was in the next room, James opened the door quickly to see Barbara sitting in an armchair in the corner.

"James my dear, I'm so glad you're okay. Please come in." Barbara smiled before rising to her feet and gave him the biggest hug you could imagine. She continued, "I know we have not much time, so I will get on with what I need to tell you. I knew about the relationship you had with Sam and at first I was angry, but now I think about it, you were made for each other. I am sorry to have lost her too, but I think you must know this." She smiled and handed James a ring.

Not knowing where this was going, James had butterflies in his stomach.

"She told me on the last day, she was going to ask you to marry her but little did she know she would get killed, none of us did. But you now need to make a decision, here is a letter from a ballet school in America, I put you and Sam forward to teach over there in a month's time as you had both proven to me that you are more than capable, and this is an acceptance letter."

James was shocked and thought carefully as he had earlier that morning considered joining the army again, if they would take him back.

"I don't know what to say, Barbara, other than thank you for everything you have done for us both, but I was considering joining the army again. I can't let them monsters get away with what they have done to Sam, I need something to make me feel like I have done the best for her and make her proud!" He looked down at the letter once more.

Barbara took his hands, “James, I have spoken with the British army, who attended the scene last night, and apparently they have caught the people who did this horrible crime, and the only war left to fight is the one that started before you even joined the forces. This is your chance to keep her memory, keep dancing, go to America and live both your dreams. That is what will make her happy and most importantly, proud. It has been a pleasure to know you and work with you, just think about it!” Barbara kissed James on the cheek and handed him a final envelope.

“Oh, before you go, here is a plane ticket to America, it was a wedding gift from Sam, she thought this would have been your happy every after! Take care, James.” She gave him one last hug and he left the house.

September 1945, the war had ended and James was back home living with Mrs Ashfield, they got along fine now and she didn’t seem to mind that James was pursuing his career in ballet. It was the 17th of September and by the front door of Mrs Ashfield’s house was a suitcase full of James’s ballet clothes, shoes, day-to-day wear, toiletries, and photographs of Sam and his family. Lying on top of the case was his overcoat, hat and plane ticket. This was it, his dream had come true but knew it would have been a lot different if the love of his life could have shared the experience with him. He said goodbye to everyone he loved and knew, leaving his life behind him, as he left for a life of ballet in America.

A year later, James was now a happier person and had started dating another woman called Michelle whom he met at a local bar in Times Square and he thought a lot of her. He was a well-established ballet dancer, teacher and performer in the United States of America; his name was well known by one and all. He had set up his own ballet school called Ashfield's, where he taught everyone, boys, girls, men and women of all ages.

Every day of the week he had his own Broadway show called 'Samantha', which portrayed how his life would have been if the love of his life was still alive, but more importantly, he was able to keep the memory of her going every night of the week in one of the world's biggest theatres.